Shadows on the Sceptered Isle

Shadows on the Sceptered Isle

JOANNE STANG

CROWN PUBLISHERS, INC.
NEW YORK

All characters portrayed in this novel are fictitious. Any resemblance to actual people is purely coincidental.

Excerpt from "After the Funeral" (in memory of Ann Jones) from *The Poems of Dylan Thomas,* copyright 1938 by New Directions Publishing Corporation. Reprinted by permission of New Directions.

Excerpt from "The Ruin" from *The Earliest English Poems,* translated by Michael Alexander (Penguin Classics, 1966), p. 30. Copyright Michael Alexander, 1966. Reprinted by permission of Penguin Books Ltd.

Inquiries should be addressed to Crown Publishers, Inc., One Park Avenue, New York, N.Y. 10016

Printed in the United States of America

Published simultaneously in Canada by General Publishing Company Limited

Library of Congress Cataloging in Publication Data

Stang, JoAnne.
Shadows on the Sceptered Isle.

I. Title.
PZ4.S7884Sh [PS3569.T332] 813'.5'4 79-19433
ISBN: 0-517-53958-6

Book design and calligraphy by Fran Nimeck Gazze

10 9 8 7 6 5 4 3 2 1

First Edition

For Arnold, with love

Shadows on the Sceptered Isle

1

They dined, and when the servants had retired, they moved into the library. Benson went through his usual routine of thumping pillows, shifting pictures, and upturning bric-a-brac.

"You're paranoid, you know that," Gamble said.

"Are you faulting me for being thorough?"

"I'm faulting you for being a perennial bore."

"You know our instructions as well as I do. One day that careless attitude of yours will . . ."

"All right!" Gamble strode to the door, opened it, looked into the hall, stepped back, and closed the door again. "All right. No one at the keyhole either. Where is he, anyway?"

"He's on the telephone."

"The project?"

"Business. New York."

"What's the drill tomorrow night?"

"The house will be full, as usual. He'll go upstairs, presumably to work, and I'll fend people off. You'll leave together. Fifteen minutes there, fifteen back, ten minutes inside. You'll have a key. An hour should be ample, even with emergencies."

"There'll be no emergencies. Why is he coming with me?"

"I don't know." Benson tapped out a cigarette and lit it. "Satisfaction?"

Before Gamble could reply, another man walked in. He moved with a deliberate tread and the blunt presumption of power; his impact on the room was marked in seconds. Gamble sat up and examined the worsted crease on his knee, knifing it with his fingers. Benson's hand trembled as he passed a briefcase across the desk.

"Never mind that," the man said, dismissing the briefcase. "Just tell me. Has it been done?"

"Yes," Benson answered.

"How many cylinders?"

"Fifty. Ten in each city."

"The sites are secure?"

"Absolutely. There's a man at each location."

"I see." He stared into an empty corner of the room. "We've begun then."

"Yes, Sir Edmund."

"Four weeks?"

"Yes, Sir Edmund."

"What do you think, Gamble?"

"Sir?"

"Will they believe us?"

"We can't be sure, sir."

"I hope they do believe us," Edmund Littell said. "For England's sake."

2

After such a long time I saw him again, through the window of a book shop in Marylebone High Street. His eyes roamed over the burnished leather bindings which covered the works of Lamb, Spenser, Wordsworth, Jane Austen, a bottle-green copy of Nelson's dispatches. The window through which he peered glistened refractively, so I had a moment to study him before he saw me standing by the wooden stall inside.

He was soberly dressed: dark coat and pants, gray scarf. His face wore its familiar look of protective detachment. It was completely blank, dead, closed, immobile—and I could not really tell whether he had, or had not, changed. Then he found me through the glass and smiled—astounded—and waved and came inside. I knew then that for me he was the same. The smile was the one I had known before—quick, white, and essentially boyish—except that it smacked of a rakish power and the pleasures of manipulation. All in all, the smile of a Mexican bandit.

"Elizabeth!"

"Michael!"

The greetings were simultaneous and we laughed. He held me at arm's length and evidenced what I took to be approval while I managed a look which was a centimeter short of being a simper. Ninny, I thought furiously. We stepped outside to be buffeted and skirted by the milling shoppers—safe, determined ladies on their way to the hairdresser or greengrocer. In the last two minutes their lives appeared to have become inexpressibly dull, and mine filled with drama. In the high recesses of my brain a tiny bell rang. "Easy now, go slow," it said. Michael frowned at the throngs.

"Let's go where we can talk."

We crossed the wet pavement to a coffeehouse filled with steam, copper vats, and sumptuous aromas. From behind a case of pastry an angular hostess popped, waving a menu across the front of her black crepe dress. She studied Michael momentarily, then executed what I had once termed "the recognition routine" as if she'd been programmed for it. Faint creases of puzzlement appeared on her forehead, followed by a swift intake of breath. The eyes widened and the jaw dropped. Michael was too accustomed to the syndrome to take much notice of it. With a grip on my elbow he steered around her, through a sea of bitty tables to a snug and quiet corner at the rear.

His back to the assorted stares, he plied me with questions. How was I? What work was I doing? How did I happen to be in London? I fingered gloves, cream, brimming cup as I answered. I was in London on sabbatical, working on research for my thesis. "I teach school now, you know," I added, then could have kicked myself in reproach. Why had I sounded so defensive?

His expression never changed—the triumph of training, I thought. He was totally engrossed in everything I had to say, a facet of him which I remembered well, but to which I had to readjust. Michael's absorption in the lives of his friends was nearly legendary. Since the first day I'd met him in the dun-hued hall of an East Side brownstone, he'd had a prickly curiosity about anyone who crossed his path.

When I was nineteen and in every sense an awkward girl—sincerely reared, overprotected, and ignorant—with a boxlike little life I thought emancipated—he hung on every word that burbled out of me. It was a form of psychological imprinting. His own existence had no room for little hopes and tiny failures, for unrewarded hungers, or for the cozy inglenooks of domesticity. He learned about all these from friends.

The spring we met he was the newest, youngest, and most skillful star on the Broadway stage and I was inhabiting my first apartment. I had fled college after my freshman year in a tumult of independence. Since "dropping out" had become unfashionable again, my parents' bewilderment was understandable. Months of carping, however, had rewarded me with the key to a dark little Manhattan chamber with an alley view and legions of cockroaches who marched into my kitchenette the minute the first-floor lunchroom closed its greasy doors. I was blissful. Outside, life teemed on all the avenues and the buildings—espaliered against the sky—were a glorious sight as I walked to work.

It was on the narrow staircase of this brownstone, then, where I met Michael Grandville. Collided with him, actually, while ensnared in a rug I'd been hauling upward. Michael bounded into this debacle, packed the rug up to my apartment, introduced himself as the fourth-floor tenant, and left. The following Sunday I found myself staring at his picture in the drama section of the *New York Times,* over columns of huzzahs about his latest performance. At our next meeting my tones were riddled with awe, which he kindly ignored and asked me to lunch. In a week we were friends, in a month I was immersed in a romance so intense that my feelings seesawed hourly from fright to wild exhilaration.

I was pitifully unprepared for such a surge of emotion. I knew Michael was a complex man. He was also tormented by pressures which I could not fathom: doubts about that epic talent, perhaps, and worry over where it would lead him. But he galloped through a life I'd only dreamed about—and his walk, his glance, his whole physical presence were so overwhelming that I'd cast my barely burgeoning maturity to the winds. I thought my love would temper all his problems.

Long afterwards, I wondered what had attracted Michael to *me*. I was, I supposed, pretty enough—in a fair, round, undemanding way. Also, Michael loathed dissemblers and I suffered an inability to tell anything but the truth. So—simple honesty, a lack of affectation, a deluge of postadolescent adoration—the ingredients were present, plus the time and place. Poor Michael. He needed a woman and what he found—or perhaps in his own insecurity had *chosen*—was yet another girl.

One day in June I came back from a weekend with my parents to find the apartment filled with flowers. White peonies, tuberoses, and freesia bloomed on every table. Propped against one vase was a note from Michael. He had gone to Hollywood to make a movie, and would write. No letter ever came. I stumbled through the next few months, going through the motions of my life, walking through the hot streets to the office and back to the brownstone again. In September I closed the apartment and went to a new school—a college well away from New York City.

Now he sat across a coffee-ringed and rather battered table from me—this dark, charming stranger—asking what I'd been doing with the last nine years. He spoke, stopped, then spoke again.

"Look, Elizabeth," he said. He examined the patina etched on a stainless spoon as if it held a code for spanning time and mending wounds. "Forgive me for leaving you that way. I was so fouled up that summer I didn't know what I was doing. I came back to New York in the fall and tried to find you, but you'd gone."

"Michael, don't." I touched his sleeve. "That was a long time ago. I've heard—I know you haven't had an easy time."

And he hadn't. There'd been an initial wave of glory—some breathtaking performances, an Academy award, several international productions—then overnight he'd seemed awash in troubles. The glowing, exotic girl who became Mrs. Michael Grandville had emerged a devout hysteric. There'd been a quick divorce. A series of ineffectual roles, done to pay off old contracts, garnered bad notices. There was word that he was solitary, moody, argumentative on the set.

Then he'd simply disappeared—packed up and left a mansion in the Santa Monica Mountains, a string of sports cars, three dogs, two horses, and a thoroughly bewildered attorney who had to dispose of it all. Subsequent reports of him had dribbled in. Michael Grandville had been seen in a Thai temple, at a Marrakesh bazaar, on an Indian reservation near Tucson. His elusiveness was a prod to the press, his absence an enigma to his public. Finally Michael Grandville had become visible only in the shadowy, nether world of his movie roles, and critics mourned that his gift had been cut off—at will.

But he was smiling at me again, and I suddenly realized that he looked remarkably well. Happy, in fact.

"You look happy."

"What?"

"Michael, you look fit and happy and—I can't express it—excited, somehow."

He laughed and reached across the table to take both my hands in his. "Well, it isn't generally known, but I guess it's really no secret. I'm working again."

"Working?"

"Not as an actor. I'm finished with that. I'm doing a documentary series for a television network in the States. Producing and directing," he grinned, "with a lot of help."

"A series? Here?"

"All over England. It will explain modern Britain in terms of its people—a young teacher from Northumberland, a Buckinghamshire farmer, a Devon innkeeper, and one titled tycoon."

"It sounds wonderful."

He grimaced. "I'll believe it when I have it all shot and in the can. It's not been quite as simple as I make it sound. We're running into some odd problems and I had a devil of a time getting financing. The industry has typecast me as a sulky, unprincipled brute."

There was silence.

"For some valid reasons, I think," Michael added.

I made a small sound of protest. "I think they were sorry to see your talent . . ." I stopped. I did not want to say the word "wasted."

"Talent be damned," Michael said coldly. "Elizabeth, if there's anything I've learned in the last few years it's that *discipline* is the most important thing in my life. Probably in anybody's life. The other thing I've learned is that I may be a good actor . . . but acting doesn't make me happy. It makes me feel like a cog, a commodity, like a robot at the end of a string. This project is the first thing I've been enthusiastic about since . . . ," his smile was reminiscent and tender, "since those first days in New York."

I stared at him. All I could think was, Why is this happening now? Why couldn't we have met again when I was twenty-three, or even twenty-five? At twenty-eight I was still fair and blonde, my face decidedly unlined, my figure slimmer, but so much gaiety, spontaneity, *warmth* even, had withered into caution. After Michael all my beaus had been disappointments. I never gave them a chance to be anything else.

Books became my solace—books and scholarship. Wounded, I sought refuge in classrooms and libraries. My first days back at the university were miserable—semesters streamed ahead and I was obsessed with getting through them. But dogged application gleaned something that surprised me: satisfaction.

Nothing dramatic, nothing intoxicating—just the quiet pleasure of work well done and the glow of academic recognition. Plus a dividend I treasured as my credits grew and Manhattan receded: the absence of pain. At the end there was a degree with honors—then graduate school—then my job. My job was now my life—my work at the Langley School.

The school had been educating the daughters of the very rich for generations. Each spring the limousines of applicants would glide down the winding roads, ebony blurs against the foliage. From these stepped cherished progeny with immaculate and famous names, and from these—in turn—would be culled a few favored candidates. My pupils.

Not only academically prestigious but architecturally perfect, an enclave of historic houses set in a gem of a New England village, glossed with the patina of Old Money, secure as the Massachusetts hills which rolled behind it, Langley was a dream school. Philippa Langley was now an ancient, ramrod creature, but her precepts encircled the school like a vise. It was a fortress of such propriety that the young fled every weekend to New York, Boston, and other playgrounds.

I was, I thought, contented there. If there was anything Miss Langley prized, it was scholarship, and I had bent my will to *that* task. How raw I must have seemed to her practiced eye when I first appeared at the school! Raw, but with a gift for teaching which she skillfully appraised. My girls worked joyfully at the assignments I gave them—ones which outlined the panoplied grandeurs of British history back through the Tudors and Plantagenets to its primitive tribal days.

Miss Langley was ambitious for me and for the credit I would ultimately bring to the school. "Take a sabbatical," she told me crisply one late spring afternoon. We were having tea in her study. Sunlight dappled the cerulean Aubusson at her feet and the paper-thin teacup rattled in her fragile hands. "Take some time off to research your dissertation, then you can come back and finish your doctorate. It's rather an endurance test, but the struggle will be good for you. So will the change of scenery. It doesn't do to grow *too* inward, my dear. I know."

I'd flushed. "But the time . . ."

"The degree is worth the time," Miss Langley stood up, her slight frame erect. "Then you can think about a book."

"A book! But Miss Langley, I hardly think . . ."

"That's your problem at the moment. You've hardly thought at all about what your future will be like. You don't appear to be interested in marriage, and if you're committed to an academic life, you'd better have a lot of projects planned. Otherwise, my dear," her watery blue eyes sought mine, "you're going to be lonely."

I'd reviewed the conversation often, principally on the late-night flight that winged from Kennedy Airport to London. The preceding weeks had been busily spent—shopping, packing, setting up a skein of correspondence which would link me to a tutor in Boston. Suddenly I was alone and on my way, enveloped in the warmth of an airline blanket, a pillow beneath my head, the sea a black and fathomless expanse thousands of feet below the plane.

I'd tried to sleep but the questions intruded. Had I already committed myself to a teacher's life, one as patently isolated as Miss Langley's? Was this trip that wise old woman's way of pushing me out into the world again—before rigidity and an "inward" tack suffocated my chances for a deep human relationship?

I thought of the school in winter—at dusk—when a kind of New England alpenglow lit the terrain. Lights would pop on in the family cottages, the homes of Langley's male staff. I'd often stopped in the quadrangle on those evenings—my breath frosty, my arms filled with books—trying to imagine the scenes inside. Father, mother, children circling the supper table, a barking dog, a crying baby, pots in the sink, boots in a puddle at the doorway. I would turn then and walk quickly across to my own apartment, unlocking the door, letting myself into the utter peace of my little parlor. I'd look at the polished copper and the old lamps so carefully acquired, the books in perfect order, the cushions plumped, no sounds at all except the sounds I made myself. How I loved it. It was solitude I saved my sweet nostalgia for. Perhaps Miss Langley was right.

"Elizabeth!"

I blinked and refocused, like someone stirring from a trance. Michael looked concerned.

"You were miles away. You're looking tired. Would you like to go back to your hotel now?"

"Oh, no! Really Michael, I'm enjoying this. It's wonderful to see you again. I'm just overwhelmed by London at the moment." And by this giddy business of feeling so alive, I thought.

"Let's have some more coffee then," he summoned some with the briefest wave, "and pastry. Would you like another pastry? No? Then drink up while it's hot and tell me about your research."

"There's not much to tell because I've only just begun. I teach at the Langley School. Outside Boston."

"I've heard of it. Posh."

"Maybe, but the curriculum is rigorous enough. My field is British history, particularly the Dark Age. You know—that period between the Romans' departure and Alfred the Great."

"I'm familiar with it."

"That makes you practically unique—to most people it's a blank. It stretched from the middle of the fifth century to the ninth, but the first two hundred years are lost—no written records, no monuments, few ruins. In the late 1930s vestiges of an Anglo-Saxon civilization began to turn up in excavations throughout Britain—at Sutton Hoo, Winchester, Glastonbury, and other spots. Some of the finds were spectacular and stirred a lot of interest in the period. There are many more digs now—traces of King Arthur are being sought from Cornwall and Somerset all the way up to Scotland."

Michael smiled. "Good old Arthur."

"I'm afraid he wasn't the Tennyson stalwart of your boyhood dreams. Probably more an ancient war lord."

"I suppose I can come to terms with that."

"At any rate, so little is known about the period that the usual investigative chronology has been reversed. Normally archeologists get their clues from the historical knowledge of an era, depend on that knowledge for dating their finds. In the case of the British Dark Age, the historians are trying to piece together a picture of those centuries from clues the archeologists have rather recently dug up. Essentially, that's what my paper will be on—the reversal of this tradition and how in the next fifty years or so we may have a fairly accurate chronology. In terms of the historical glimmerings already arrived at, of course."

"That was very crisply done."

"Crisply!"

"Sweetheart, you astound me. Who would have thought that . . ."

"That I could have managed to educate myself? Really Michael, I hate to accuse you of male chauvinism but . . ."

"She bristles too! Would you like me to say you're beautiful when you're angry? That worked in the flicks."

"The flicks of the thirties, I think. Don't tease me, Michael. I'm serious about my work."

"Indeed you are, love, and you should be. Forgive me. It's just not the way I remembered you."

We both fell into silence at that, I cataloguing the irrevocably departed years, Michael musing over I knew not what—his brow furrowed, his fingers drumming on the tabletop. His demeanor had altered. He was troubled now. I knew the symptoms. When something nagged at him, he got restless.

Abruptly, he leaned toward me. "What would you think if I asked you . . ." There was the faintest giggle at my elbow. We turned. There stood two ladies who wore upon their heads what appeared to be inverted flowerpots, one pink and one pistachio. In contrast to the concave hostess they were pleasantly bombé, and their middle-aged faces held beseeching puppies' eyes. Michael rose.

One spoke. "Mr. Grandville, may we have your autograph?" She held out pen and paper.

Michael smiled, then with all suitable gravity inquired, "Just one? May I write one for each of you?" The heads bobbed yes, and he wrote chirpy blips to Rose and then to Sybil.

He stood politely while they backed away, then sat and began rummaging through his pockets, his eyes scanning the check. "Let's go," he said. His voice was testy. I knew he chafed at the claptrap rigmarole of fame—"notoriety" he'd called it—but even so, he seemed inordinately tense. He held my coat while I slipped into it.

Outside it was raining in earnest. Michael put up my umbrella and we walked around the corner and down the convolutions of Marylebone Lane, past florists' stalls, antique shops, and a few rather gummy boutiques. Unprotected pedestrians scurried along close to the buildings, a few hardy souls paused to browse. We plodded, Michael saying nothing, I at a half-trot beside him. I felt the backs of my stockings grow clammy, along with my raincoat hem.

We reached a gourmet cookware emporium just as its lights popped on. I slowed and stepped inside the doorway, warmed by the sight of endearing objects like wooden spoons and steamers. Michael hesitated for a moment, then quite deliberately put down the umbrella, and moved in front of me.

He stood close. The damp front of his coat had a wet-wool smell. Over his shoulder I could see the hanging crepe pans, a nest of bains-maries, some shiny escargotieres, a tall glass filled with paper flutings. Lightheaded, I tried to stay detached, but the old feelings flooded back—the rampant heartbeat, shallow breathing, and wobble knees. Michael was saying something. His hands held my arms. I heard the words and looked at him in disbelief. He stared down, his grip tightened, and he repeated, "Elizabeth, will you help me?"

3

A taxi wheeled into the lane just then, tootling, teetering slightly, and squeaking on the curve. The driver was hunched over the wheel, obviously hell-bent for the garage and home. Waving the umbrella, Michael shouted at him, pulled me into the street, ignored some sour looks, and shoved me into the cab.

"We'll never find another at the rush hour, and we can't talk in doorways, can we? Where are you staying?" I told him of the Hotel Douglass, which sat in a tiny road off the end of Sloane Street. He gave some expert directions to the driver, leaned back on the cold leather seat, noticed I was shivering, and flung a casual arm around my shoulders. I felt like a plastic tiddleywink, diddled for a time atop a geyser, then set flat. London sped by, flashes of light and the red sheen of buses. We whirled around Hyde Park Corner, along Knightsbridge, down Sloane Street, turned a final corner and pulled up in front of the hotel.

The Douglass was much favored by visiting academics who no doubt found in its shabby Persians and thin-napped upholstery a faithful replica of their digs at home. At the end of its long front hall there was a tiny television lounge, which we looked into. It was empty and the television set, which a few hours later would be wreathed in pipe smoke, stared blank and implacable across the room. Michael started the electric fire in the minuscule grate, then walked back down the hall to get some sherry. I drew off my sodden shoes and pulled the toes of my damp nylons away from my numbed feet.

"Have some." Michael was back with the sherry. I sipped it gratefully.

"I seem to have spent the last few hours being plied with liquids."

"None of them wild intoxicants, however." Michael stretched long legs toward the fire, then turned to look at me.

"What I started to ask you . . . what I'm going to say . . . may seem outlandish, Elizabeth. I think the easiest way to explain it all is to begin at the beginning, which is about three years ago." He paused, assembling his thoughts, and then went on. "I felt I was finished then, not just as an actor, but as a man. I'd gone to Hollywood confident I could handle the pressures. I thought I could manage to be my own person anywhere, but I was wrong. I couldn't. I won't make a lot of pretentious excuses. In five years I managed to fail at marriage and run my career into the ground.

"When I left I suppose I was about as spiritually bankrupt as a human being can be, but what really grated was the knowledge that I hadn't been proud of my work in a long, long time. We're all funny creatures, Elizabeth. I think most of us can take a considerable amount of abuse or deprivation if our central core remains intact—if inside we know we have a gift—a craft—we can take out and wave at the world. Well, my craft was gone. I'd squandered it. There's a word to describe the way I felt. It's an unfashionable word in these Freudian times, but it suits my condition. I felt like a bum."

"Michael . . ."

"No, sweetheart. Please hear me out. I flitted around for a while, then came to England—to Wales—to a village in Denbighshire. It was a tiny place where I'd been on location before—a backdrop for one of those period epics I had to do. I was struck by its remoteness, and its peace. The whole town has twelve houses, a general store, a pub, and a gas pump, surrounded by a clump of green hills. I took a cottage and for months did nothing but sleep and walk. There were rumors of a nervous breakdown. Well, it was not as dramatic as that, but there's no doubt that in every sense I was healing myself.

"The townspeople were marvelous. I was staggered by their decency. They'd certainly been to the movies, or had been exposed to films on television, and I could hardly walk around with a paper bag over my head. They knew who I was all right, but they left me alone. I must have seemed every kind of eccentric, too—brooding off in that stone hut—yet nobody questioned my behavior. Beyond the ordinary transactions—buying the daily paper, stocking up on supplies—there were no verbal exchanges at all. I might have been invisible. I suppose it's odd to be enamored of reticence, but I came to love this country. Britain seemed to me about the last place on earth where people seemed really tolerant, where being different was not considered a kind of crime.

"When I began feeling myself again," Michael smiled, "I began taking the odd trip down to London to see friends. One of them, a fellow named David Cheney, suggested a project that seemed impractical at first, but then I began to warm up to the idea. David is a playwright . . ."

"Oh yes, I know of him. I saw one of his plays—*The Treasure House*—when it ran in Boston last year."

"Right. He's immensely talented, and a paradox in a way. He has this wild imagination in his work, but privately he's very settled, very methodical. 'Mike, old boy,' he said to me, 'you need a planned pursuit. You've got to get with it in some way or other. The sooner you do, the better you'll feel.'

"What he suggested was this TV series. It seemed to have all the requirements—a chance to live and work in England, and a hope of creating something I could be proud of. At first I protested that I hadn't the know-how, but then I found that you can hardly work in motion pictures without picking up *some* expertise—and since I was going to be the producer, I could hire the strategic men, like scriptwriters and cameramen. I also found my name still has some drawing power with those who pay the bills. It wasn't easy, but I got the contracts and the money.

"And . . ." Michael stood up, walked to the window, and with his back toward me, shrugged. "Everything was going well until last week," he turned, "when we ran into trouble with our pièce de résistance."

"With whom?"

"Sir Edmund Littell—industrialist and financial whiz. Not very well known in America, and a rather private person even here, considering his status. He's the head of Marchant's, Limited."

"The chemical firm."

"Yes. Started by his father in the late twenties to produce disinfectants and now a worldwide conglomerate with plants and research laboratories around the world. They make everything from pesticides to bathing-suit fibers."

"What's the problem with Sir Edmund?"

"He's balking, and if he won't let us shoot, we're in trouble."

"Can't you get someone else?"

"Perhaps, but I'd hate to—for several reasons. Littell is really the pivotal figure in the series. We've geared everything else to build up to him. The other characters are average people—'just folks' you might say—and Sir Edmund was chosen to give American audiences some insights into how the titled British live. We picked him because he touches all bases. He's an international financial figure and a totally modern British executive, who happens to be deeply rooted in the past."

"By lineage, you mean?"

"By lineage *and* avocation. Sir Edmund is the director of the Society for Saxon Archeology."

"Oh."

"Exactly." Michael waved his empty glass. "Since I've led you this far down the well-known path, would you like a refill before I continue?"

"I can do without at the moment. Go on."

"The Littell homestead, if you can call it that, is down in Somerset, a charming little place with twenty-six bedrooms."

"Michael!"

"Not all occupied, of course. Behind the estate is a village, built originally to house retainers I imagine, but now only partly owned by the Littells. Behind *that* is Thorn Hill, a three hundred-foot-high earthwork, probably Iron Age. According to legend, it got its name when some Celtic saint climbed its thorn-covered sides in his bare feet, to plant his staff at the summit. There's also an early church, eighth century perhaps."

"You're beginning to sound highly expert yourself."

"I've been going over the research with the writer. Thorn Hill is the perfect backdrop for this sequence—a unique one, really. Finding something else as good could cost us months."

It was almost night, and the meager light from the courtyard had diminished to the point where Michael's frame had blurred. I crossed the room in my stockinged feet to snap on a lamp and when I turned back he was hunched over, elbows on knees, his hands rubbing his eyes in weariness and frustration. I remembered that I'd seen him so once before—in my little apartment. It had been evening then too, and he'd just finished reading a script which had come—heavily mottled with postal insignia—from his agent on the Coast. Apparently it had been terrible, or perhaps its origin seemed ominous. Anyway, Michael had adopted the same posture, and on that occasion I had laid my hand upon his head. I found I could not do so now. I waited.

Presently he looked up. His words were noncommittal, but his eyes were bleak. "It's quite an impasse, you know."

I sat on the lumpen hassock next to his chair and said, "Tell me the rest."

Michael sighed. "Sir Edmund's great enthusiasm is an archeological dig which he's been conducting at Thorn Hill for two years now. He's using a considerable crew of university undergraduates, most of them on leave from school, I think. I don't know what they expect to find, Saxon battlements, probably. Sir Edmund's terribly proud of the effort. The hill is something of a family shrine.

"At first Littell seemed interested in doing the film. We promised to treat the dig with respect, and he liked the idea that we chose to emphasize the responsibilities of title. We made a preliminary trip down to Somerset to reserve some lodgings and line up the work. Sir Edmund was supposed to let me know when I could bring the whole crew there. He's been stalling me for ten days now, and I can't find out why.

"Maybe he feels we're hairy show-business types who will muck up the excavation, maybe he's just being perverse, or maybe my alluring reputation has preceded me. Whatever the reason, without him I'm sunk. I can't get the rest of the money unless he cooperates, I can't afford to keep the crew on salary while we wait, yet I can't let them go either. They're a crackerjack bunch and it would be hellish to assemble another group of the same quality."

"You say he's not been heavily publicized?"

"No. His personal appearances have been limited to rather stuffy occasions—industrialists' dinners or commercial fairs where Marchant's products were displayed. And I suppose he has some activities as a publisher. He has a little publishing house there in the village. It grinds out books and pamphlets on British archeology—sort of a cottage industry."

"Also Thorn Hill-based. The whole arrangement seems so—I don't know—sort of sheltered and insular."

"Probably is. Anyway, he's having a gathering at his London house tonight to which I'm invited. I think in the course of the evening he's going to tell me that he's ever-so-sorry, but he finds he'll be unavailable for the next six months—a pressing merger or a world trip."

"Would he do that, Michael?"

"There's no reason why he shouldn't. He has no commitment to me other than a verbal one. I guess it was naïve of me to take him at his word when he first agreed to do the film. I just never thought he'd renege." He looked grim. "It's bad. I can't afford another failure."

The next move was mine. I could step away from this moment as effortlessly as I glided through my life at home. No one would chastise me for preferring to be uninvolved. Michael would grapple with his problem and somehow solve it. I would remain a spectator. Participants got hurt—not bodily perhaps—but in ways that were often harder to bear. A few words and he would go away. I could write my paper and go back to Langley. Untouched. Unmoved. The warning bells in my head were sounding in unison now—a cacophony that chimed for naught.

"Michael." I leaned toward him. "How can I help?"

His relief was obvious. "You could be a *great* help, Elizabeth, and I don't think it would take too much of your time—a week or two at most. I thought of it while we were talking in the café. Your background's perfect, and you might find Thorn Hill useful in your own work. I'd like you to be my technical adviser."

"I don't understand. Adviser in what way?"

"I thought you might come with me to Sir Edmund's tonight. I'd introduce you as someone the company had engaged to frame the dig in a proper light—a scholarly light. You're an expert of a kind on the period, and your credentials are excellent—the Langley School is well known everywhere. If I could show Littell that we hired someone who could translate his precious excavation into glorious film, backed by an impeccable commentary, he might let me go ahead."

"But Michael, I know *nothing* about film."

"You don't have to. Your job is to make sure the script is faithful to the historical facts and to be present during the shooting to make sure this perspective is maintained. Look, it's no more complicated than what you do every day in your classes. You won't have any homework, beyond reading the script—our writer will work with you on revisions. He'd welcome the company I think—he's up to his hips in Saxon kings."

We laughed aloud at this—the coconspirators—then Michael wheeled about, pacing up and down the room, talking as he walked, ebullient, gesturing, detailing plans for the filming.

"Stop. Wait!" I caught his arm. "What on earth do I say to Sir Edmund?"

"In two words—very little. I'll tell him all about you. I'm sure he won't get into anything very technical, not at this meeting anyhow. On other occasions—if there *are* other occasions—you'll be busy working." He reached up to tuck an errant strand of hair behind my ear. "Trust me, Beth. I won't involve you in an embarrassment."

I hardly knew what to say. He seemed to be waiting for a word of confidence, an endorsement, for the reprise of a time when I adored and didn't question. He was seeking a girl who didn't exist anymore. We both knew that, but I was too cowardly to confirm it. I stepped backward and turned to pick up my shoes, my bag, and my still-damp raincoat. When I looked at him again he had rearranged his face. His glance was fond—and brotherly.

"Littell is giving us supper." He looked at his watch. "It's seven-fifteen now. My flat's about ten blocks from here. I'll walk over, change, and be back in an hour. Suit you?"

"Fine."

We walked down the hall together. He left with an absent-minded pat on my shoulder and I'm sure I seemed equally distracted. A swarm of possibilities were whirling through my mind—none of them especially reassuring. Upstairs I bathed in a claw-foot tub, rested briefly, brushed my hair, and put on a navy blue dress of slithery fabric, but circumspect style. I tucked some essentials into my purse, and then the phone rang. It was the desk, announcing Michael. In a china dish on the bureau lay a slender bracelet, a sliver of Peruvian silver he had given me that memorable summer. I'd kept it long after hope had faded, after Michael had become a phantom figure on the fringe of the news photos, caught as he ran from place to place. I slipped it on my wrist and then stared down at it.

My God, I thought. What have I done?

4

Gamble parked midway up the row, doused the car lights, and walked briskly toward the cul-de-sac. The street was quiet and contained: Edwardian streetlamps lit the mellowed brick façades of its seven houses. Their occupants were at dinner or away; three houses sat in darkness. Jock Magee's door was the last; there was a light upstairs. Magee's white Rolls-Royce stood in the circle, blocking the turn.

Gamble slipped the key into the lock, turned it, and stepped inside. The hall and the flight of stairs that faced him were lushly carpeted. He ran up, not touching the bannister. There were three closed doors in the upper hall and he stood there, hoping to hear a sound. There was none, so he considered the doors. The one at the end was narrower, probably a bath. The next would be an adjoining bedroom and the nearest door might be a study. He decided to chance that door and hoped that Magee was not only behind it, but far from a window.

There were two pieces of luggage just inside and a bottle of Scotch on a table. Beside them, Magee lay sprawled on a couch fast asleep, his skinny arms flung out. His mouth hung open, and the coarse features looked uglier in repose. Gamble leaned one knee into the couch and took out the knife, then grasped a throw pillow with his left hand. He pressed the cold blade against the sallow cheek, and bent down to Magee's ear.

"Jock," he whispered. "Jock, wake up."

Magee stirred.

"Wake up, Jock. I have a surprise here."

Magee's eyes opened. Gamble put the pillow over his mouth.

"Are you awake, Jock? I'm going to kill you now."

Magee's eyes widened and his body heaved, but Gamble drove in the knife before he could struggle. He held it in until the body sagged, then pulled out Magee's silk shirt and cleaned the blade on its surplus. He wiped all the knobs on the way out.

The car's other occupant leaned from its shadowed rear towards the driver's seat. "Any trouble?"

"None. He was sleeping."

"Sleeping!"

Gamble smiled in the darkness; he knew the next question.

"Did you wake him?"

"Yes, sir."

"He knew what was happening?"

"Yes."

"Good," said Sir Edmund.

5

When we arrived the rain had stopped and only the finest mist lay over Sir Edmund's house and the tiny park it faced. The house was Adam-like in some respects: Corinthian pilasters divided the upper stories, a handsome fan window arched over the door. The tone was subdued, however, more severe than elegant. We rang and the door was opened by a stocky, flush-faced man in a dark suit, holding both a glass and a small notebook in his left hand. Perspiration shone on his upper lip and his balding head.

"Good evening. Come in, Mr. Grandville. Sir Edmund's in conference, but he should be down shortly. Someone . . ." He turned as a maid appeared. "Ah yes. Maria will take your things and show you inside. I'll be back as soon as I can." He smiled at me. "Happy to see you both."

"Who is he?" I whispered to Michael.

"John Benson. Sir Edmund's secretary—a whirlwind, but a very discreet one."

"I think he believes we've met before."

"I promise you I've not brought another blue-eyed blonde to this house. Only brunettes."

"You're very amusing this evening."

The hall was Italianate—black-and-white-flagged-marble floors, a white-marble staircase with delicate wrought-ironwork. Two portraits held eighteenth-century ladies—their chiffons blowing, clouds lowering behind, as if they'd sprung from some celestial province.

Maria ushered us into the drawing room, peopled by thirty-odd who were eating, drinking, smoking, and conversing in the intricate minuet of the townhouse party. The ceiling was very high, its plasterwork exquisite. There was a Chinese Chippendale mirror, a lovely lacquered screen, a Constable landscape, and an ornately carved chimneypiece. Crystal tinkled on proffered trays, bowls of flowers were everywhere. The room thrummed, but in a muted, polished vein which no single voice preempted. I sat on the edge of an aubergine sofa while Michael—smiling, nodding—eased himself into the cadence of the group. Two minutes inside the house and I felt lost. When Michael pointed to the buffet and held out his hand, I was glad to move through the guests to a candlelit table. There a covey of servants tended the pâtés and béchameled breasts, the galantines and mousses.

My plate was half full when a hand clamped upon my shoulder. I turned to find a tall man looking down at me. His other arm hung around Michael's neck. Amiably disheveled, his tweed jacket worn to the nub, brown hair as long and curly as a child's after a summer swim, he'd naturally acquired a much-emulated London "look"—he was fashionably tattered.

"Elizabeth," Michael said, "I'd like you to meet David Cheney. David, this is Elizabeth Kendall."

"A great pleasure, Miss Kendall," Cheney's hand enveloped mine. "I'd no idea Michael had a compatriot in the wings."

"We met again this afternoon. Unexpectedly."

"Life is full of surprises. A very pleasant one, in this case."

"Thank you."

"Er—David," Michael waved a fork. "Have some food."

"Not now," Cheney scanned the crowd. "Have you seen Lily?"

"No. Are you sure she's supposed to be here?"

"Old friend," Cheney's tone was wry, "can you imagine me present without that prospect? I'll have a look around." He smiled at me, said, "Enjoy yourself," and moved away.

"Who's Lily?"

"Felicia Littell. Lily for short. She's Sir Edmund's daughter."

"Is David her boyfriend?"

"David has had to get in line. She's lively, Lily is—and a budding actress to boot. Just now she has a part in David's new play. If Lily has three lines she'll need four weeks of coaching to get them right."

"Isn't that out of character? For David, I mean. He seems so professional."

"He is, but he's crazy about the girl. He thinks the responsibility of giving a performance will infuse her with some kind of maturity. A pipe dream. Naturally he'll see that she's acceptable in the part, and God knows she's decorative. The critics will like that. I'm making a prediction right now."

"A prediction?"

"Yes. I think David will work her until those three lines glow, but she'll quit the show in about ten days."

"Even if her notices are good?"

"Even if the notices imply she's Duse reborn. She simply hasn't the staying power to perform night after night for months. There'll be a row, and David will pack up what's left of his dignity and retreat. Hastily. He's smitten, but not drugged."

I stared up at Michael. His smile had a flinty edge. "You're awfully hard on her."

"Haven't you noticed? I've developed a pious impatience

with anyone who won't do his job. Takes one to know one. Anyway . . ." He stopped. "There he is. Sir Edmund." Michael inclined his head toward a man just entering, then brushed his lips across my forehead. "They're playing our music, dearest. Wish me luck." The flinty smile returned, he took a deep breath and started across the room.

Sir Edmund's broad forehead and large brown eyes reminded me of someone else. His auburn hair was full, graying at the temples, and his moustache had a cindery cast. He was of medium height but—like many men with barrel chests—looked shorter. Then I knew. In doublet and with an added beard he would have been a twin to William Byrd, the Elizabethan composer of masses and motets. At that point he stepped forward to greet Michael and the polyphonic chorus vanished. The gesture had been clipped and military. An interesting ambivalence.

I was too far removed to hear, so I tried to fathom snippets of their conversation via body English. Sir Edmund stood sober and attentive. Michael seemed involved in nonstop speech—only one involuntary, twitchy movement of his head gave evidence of his tension. I could hardly stand there bug-eyed for long, so I accepted a demitasse and settled next to a gelid creature in total black who regaled me with a litany on the treachery of hairdressers. I had the feeling she'd recited it often. She was reveling in the perils of an apricot tint when Michael came back.

"He wants to meet you."

"Oh."

"Put your cup down, sweetheart."

"Oh, yes. Of course." I stood up and my stomach promptly thunked to what seemed to be knee level. Sir Edmund was looking at me from behind a blur of guests. Silly, I thought. He looks perfectly civil. Why be timid about meeting him?

Sir Edmund's greeting was distant but correct. "I'm happy to meet you, Miss Kendall. Mr. Grandville has told me of your interests. I hope you won't be disappointed in Saxon England. There's so little left."

"I'm pleased to be here, Sir Edmund. Seeing everything first-hand is very exciting."

"Undoubtedly. What *have* you seen, so far?"

"Well, I've just been in England a week, but I've been up to Northamptonshire, to the church at Earls Barton."

"Ah, yes."

"And I've spent two afternoons in the British Museum, looking at the Sutton Hoo treasure."

"I see. Well, those are the more spectacular Saxon examples, of course. I'm afraid the rest tends to be bits and pieces and—where the Dark Age is concerned—crumbs. How ever did you become attached to such a desolate period?"

Coming from Sir Edmund, the question surprised me. Miss Langley had once hinted that fifth-century Britain was an odd and maybe morbid focus. I'd found it hard to explain my fascination with the shadowy mists of the era—the crumbling Roman villas, embattled Britons and exultant invaders: men who'd swirled across the land, spiked-iron spears in their heathen fists.

"I don't know really . . ." I faltered. "I find it very poignant, somehow. A time when Englishmen seemed terribly . . ."

"Bereft?"

"Yes. A sad, lost time in history."

"Many share your view, but perhaps there were more glories then than now. It's hard to hope for the human condition at the moment. Our cities seem equally besieged."

An appropriate group of words came to mind, and without thinking much, I said them. "My tents are fallen, my trumpets and the sweet sound/of my harps is silent on my clouded hills."

I was astonished to see twin glints of moisture appear in Sir Edmund's brown eyes. "Blake. An authentic prophet. It's gratifying to hear him quoted." He paused. "Many people come to England for rather superficial purposes, Miss Kendall. I think, however, that your visit will be fruitful."

He stepped back. Three paces away John Benson had been waiting for an interruption. He moved forward, a sheaf of messages in his hand. I felt Michael's fingers on my elbow. The audience was over.

Michael walked me back across the room, calm on the surface, charged beneath. "We were speaking of performances a while ago," he said. "May I say yours was perfect?"

"It wasn't a performance. I rather like him."

"While he was talking to you he actually seemed human. All I got was a fishy stare."

"Does that mean no film?"

"I don't know. The reception was lukewarm but his questions were heartening. He asked about our schedule, how long the filming would take, how many in crew, what kind of equipment we'd use. Knowledgeable, specific questions."

"But?"

"But he gave no commitment, not even a clue to when I might expect an answer. Beth, I'm sorry to leave you again, but would you forgive me? I want to find David and get his reaction. He's a trusty barometer."

"Go ahead. I'll amuse myself. Not here, though."

"Find it overpowering?"

"A bit. Is there a smaller room?"

"I think so. This way." We went back into the hall and crossed it. Michael opened a door and we stepped into a library. He pointed me toward a wing chair, executed a White Rabbit double-step, and disappeared again.

I didn't mind. Everyone's idea of heaven differs and mine was a library like this: a solid oaken refuge which put to shame the succession of chintzy havens I had created through the years. Chairs and couch were cognac leather. Books lined the wall in variegated counterpoint to paneling. A clock under glass ticked softly, but that was the only sound. I might have been alone in the house.

I began to browse through titles. There was a lot of history, most of it British. I counted thirteen books on both World Wars and the period between them. There were volumes on armor—fluted chamfrons back to primitive Celtic shields—and pamphlets on Saxon artifacts and Pictish broaches.

Down on a lower shelf, two red-bound covers caught my eye. *Burke's Landed Gentry.* Curiosity fought qualms about examining the pedigree of one's host. Curiosity won and the pedigree was formidable indeed. Edmund Mark William Henry Gambier Littell had gone to Winchester and Balliol College, Oxford. He'd spent 1940 to 1946 in the British Army—with a slew of decorations noting expertise and bravery—and a final rank of major. He'd gone back to Oxford for his degree and, in his mid-thirties, married Margaret Cazalet. A daughter was born the following year, his wife died twelve months later. He was a Fellow of the Society of Antiquaries, a Fellow of the Royal Historical Society, and chairman of a battery of archeological committees. Half Norman, the chronicled Littell ancestors went back to the twelfth century in Somerset.

Next to Burke's were a row of magazines, precisely stacked twenty-five-year-old copies of *Country Life.* The inside pages still had a fresh and glossy look. The only hint to their age were the prices in house offerings, all pittances in the current market. Had Sir Edmund and his Margaret traipsed through the English countryside, examining thatched cottages, timbered lodges, and minor Palladian villas? Had they sought a place of their own, away from Thorn Hill? I thought about Margaret Littell. She would have been sheltered and carefully educated, with one of those pressed-hibiscus English complexions, radiant with new-bride pleasures, the "right" sort of wife for Sir Edmund. Two years of marriage to a mature man, one year of motherhood, and she had died, leaving him with an empty house and a mewling baby. Sad.

A satin-bound merino shawl lay folded on a footstool near my chair, and I realized, suddenly, how weary I was. It seemed several years of electric happenings had been telescoped into one day—and that day was not over. I longed to pull the shawl's comforting warmth over my body and nap. Twenty minutes, perhaps, and I'd feel fine again. Then I realized how I'd look to someone coming into the room, wrapped like a mummified deck-chair occupant and dead to the world. Regretfully, I decided to forego the throw. I lay back, my head propped against the corner of the chair, and closed my eyes.

I was at Langley and someone was rattling my office door. Probably Sarah Boardman, who jiggled her multicharmed bracelets through every class. I'd have to remind her once more not to wear them. The rattling began again. Inconsiderate girl. Aloud, I said, "Stop that!" and then awakened. Someone was pulling the library doorknob. Pushing and pulling. A voice, low and urgent, called "Elizabeth!" I got up quickly, stiff and chilled, and went to the door.

"It's me, Elizabeth. Michael."

"Wait just a moment. The door seems to have locked itself. There!"

The bolt clicked, the door swung toward me, and Michael walked in, his arms enveloping the most beautiful girl I had ever seen. Violet eyes, now kohled by grief, shone in a whey-pale face. Taffy hair hung straight to the shoulders, framing silken cheeks and the rosebud lips were parted. The effect was pre-Raphaelite: primordial loveliness, frozen in anguish.

"It's Lily," Michael said. "Can you find some brandy?"

"I think I saw . . ." A decanter and glasses stood on a tray. "Yes. Over here. I'll pour some."

"Pour two. I need one myself." Michael sat Lily in the chair I'd just vacated and held her upright. He raised the brandy to her lips, then tipped it—expertly—down her throat. She coughed delicately and stared ahead. The door was rattling again. I opened it, and David walked in.

"Where have you been . . . ," he said, and stopped. "My God, what's the matter with her?"

"Shock, I think. I was looking for *you* and I thought you'd be with Lily. Benson said he'd seen her phoning in the sitting room upstairs. When I got there she was this way. The phone was dangling in her hand. She needs a doctor."

"We'd better call her father first." David turned toward the door.

"No." The word was like a sigh. We turned and looked at Lily. "Don't call my father. It's all right."

David sat on the chair arm and took her hand. "My darling, what happened?"

"It's Jock. He's gone."

"Jock Magee? How gone, Lily?"

"Dead and gone, David. *Dead.* They just found him. Oh, David!" The lovely face crumbled and she fell against him, sobbing.

David looked at us, aghast. "I can't believe it."

Nor could I. Jock Magee, whose voice brayed out of record shops around the world. Brilliant, irreverent, and crude, he wielded that voice with an arrogance which had mesmerized the young—and repelled almost everyone else. Dead at roughly thirty.

Lily raised her head. "I knew he'd be back from his American tour today, so I called this afternoon. There was no answer. When I called again . . . just now . . . a policeman answered. He asked me all kinds of questions . . . who was I, when had I last seen Jock . . . then he told me Jock was dead." She twisted in the chair and looked wildly up at David. "I don't understand! I don't understand!"

"Easy, Lily. Easy." David stroked her hair. "What is it? What don't you understand?"

"I don't think they meant just *dead* . . . like dead from sickness. I think . . . they think . . . that he was killed."

"No, Lily. Surely not."

"Then why ask me all those questions? Another man got on and said the police would be speaking to me later. Do they do all that in a normal death?"

"I don't know," David answered grimly, "but I'll find out. Right now I'm taking you upstairs." He pulled Lily to her feet. Her eyes had glazed again and she seemed some lifeless doll.

"Let me help."

"No, Elizabeth. I'll get Maria. We'll look after her." Hands firm on her thin shoulders, he piloted Lily toward the door. At the threshold, he turned and added. "You look tired, Elizabeth. You must have had a full evening yourself." They went out and Michael and I were left in silence, except for the ticking clock.

"I'll have a drink now," Michael said. "Pour you one?"

"Yes. Thanks." I walked to the fireplace and watched the embers. After a moment, Michael came over. He set the brandy on the mantelpiece, saying quietly, "I hope you'll forgive my shabby behavior."

"Shabby?"

"Yes. David was right. You're bone tired and I never noticed. I've been so absorbed in this idiot film that I haven't noticed much of anything lately. I know this hasn't been the day you planned."

The remark sprung from concern and from Michael's contriteness but, nevertheless, it stung. From the marginal pleasures of the British Museum Reading Room, my day would have advanced to a bookshop browse, a thrifty tea instead of dinner, and an evening in my room at the Douglass, scanning photographs of mounds and barrows in southeast Suffolk. It would have been a safe day in the safe life of a cautious young woman, and the contrasts between that programme and the events of the past six hours were too much for my creviced ego to withstand. When Michael continued, "I wouldn't blame you if you felt . . . ," I quickly filled in, ". . . used?"

He winced. "You're right, of course, Beth. I'd understand if you wanted to chuck all this."

There it was again—an "out." Fate had dealt me a reunion with someone I'd never thought I'd see again, a compelling bunch of supplementary characters, this glittering house, even an episode of sudden death. How could I now opt for a life of rubber-plant placidity?

Without wavering, I answered, "No, Michael. I said I'd help you and I will."

Michael grinned then—with his old highwayman aplomb. "In that case I should tell you that I got the word from Benson. We're in business. I'm to book rooms for the crew. They come down to Thorn Hill Monday and we . . . you and I, that is . . . leave first thing in the morning."

6

In Michael's hands the car swiveled neatly through the corkscrew route out of London, whipped along the highway and down a side road which bypassed Salisbury. The cathedral spire gleamed in the sunlight, another vista preserved, and I thought gratefully of that army of Britons who buffed church plate, spruced neglected corners, and fought creeping concrete everywhere.

The first part of our trip had been filled with chitchat, a rehash of my negotiations with the Douglass, whose manager finally found a two-by-nothing space to store the bulk of my books and my "city" clothes. I was warned there might be no vacancy when I returned, but paying for an unused room was too much pocketbook drain.

"Wise move," Michael said. "Anyway, we can always get you in somewhere. Or put you up with a friend," he added, making mince of my arrangements.

Then we'd switched to the subject of Jock Magee. The coverage in the morning paper had been lurid: the discovery of the bloodied body by Magee's manager, the search for the weapon, a recount of Jock's checkered past.

"Will they drag Lily into it?" I asked.

"Perhaps not. She's Sir Edmund's daughter after all, and it should be simple to confirm that she was at home all afternoon and evening. I'm sure there are hundreds with more reason to stab Magee than Lily. Besides, she jilted *him.*"

"Oh?"

"A fact that was immaterial to Lily. She still had him securely on the string. It's David I'm really worried about. He's more involved with Lily than I supposed. Damn that poisonous child! She'll muck up his life and crimp his output."

"Oh come on, Michael. He's a free agent, surely, and no schoolboy. He'll survive."

"Will he?" Michael turned from the wheel. "You underestimate Lily. There's a legion of slain warriors in her wake. Lawyers, doctors, journalists. Young and old. Married and unmarried. She's been at it for years."

"How old is she?"

"Chronologically? Twenty-four. If you count by experience, she's forty-five. No wonder she's upset about Jock. He's the first one who actually expired."

We were passing a village: brown houses, cottage gardens with sweet herbaceous borders, beech-lined lanes. Some rosy children raised their arms in greeting and I could hear a housewife calling to them. As we drove past her voice hung in the air behind us, liquid and pure, aloft in that sunlit space. I did not want to talk about breathtaking Lily just now, but Michael went on.

"Jock was ferocious but, near Lily, he behaved like a bleating lamb."

"She's so lovely, Michael."

"That's only part of it. Lily has a way of being irresistible. The desire to . . . to protect her, I guess . . . can be overwhelming. The hell of it is, she always chooses her successor while the current flame's still burning. The victim can only watch, helpless, while she moves on to her next attachment. Jock had to watch that way while she snared David. What I'd like to know is, who follows David?"

Who indeed, I thought.

"Somehow I think it all revolves around her father," Michael said.

"Sir Edmund? I should think he'd be an exceptional parent."

"He is, actually. The party last night, for example. I'm told he hates large groups of people, but he periodically has those gatherings in the hope Lily will meet some congenial friends."

" 'Congenial' meaning 'suitable.' "

"Right."

"I wonder who chooses the guests," I said, thinking of Apricot Tint.

"Oh, Benson probably, but it doesn't really matter. Lily makes a brief appearance, then goes up to her room and locks the door. Another nose-thumbing gesture. It's as if she hasn't punished Sir Edmund enough—or the men she goes with, for that matter."

"I don't mean to sound trite, but it seems Lily's due for some psychotherapy."

"I suppose so. I pity the analyst."

Conversation lagged for a bit, while I admired the pastoral calm of the countryside and Michael concentrated on his driving. He managed the Mercedes with the almost aimless grace of a natural athlete, circling round-abouts and swirling through market squares as if they were nonexistent. His behavior was somehow reminiscent of his Broadway appearances, particularly the final performance of his last legitimate play. Then scenery, costumes, several eloquent costars, and the surging prose of a prize-laden playwright all paled to nothing as the audience sat riveted to every gesture. It had been an exercise in audacity as well as skill, and after the bombast of the final calls, the audience had virtually tottered away. In triumph, Michael had been irritatingly casual. He'd simply washed up and gone home. Remembering, I smiled.

"It's nice to see you smile," he said.

"I thought you were watching the road."

"I have mysterious antennae which register your every mood. What were you thinking?"

"About the last performance of *Judgment Day*, and how you closed up shop that night. With such finality."

"After two-hundred-and-nine performances I was just grateful to get away. God, what a bore those last weeks were! What a bore actors are, for that matter."

"Funny, I've never thought of you that way."

"That's because I have you hypnotized, my pretty."

"Not hypnotized enough to calm my nerves. How much further is it?"

The car swerved on a wicked curve and Michael's eyes flicked at a road sign. "Less than a mile."

"Will Sir Edmund be there?"

"I expect so. I'm to go over our work plan with him. He wants to know all our moves, down to the last detail, and I'll have to give him a shooting script."

"Oh."

"There's one for you too. You can read it tomorrow. When Ian Farr . . . he's the writer . . . comes down on Monday, you can both work on revisions. There are bound to be a few, there always are."

"Suppose Sir Edmund hates the present script and wants it completely rewritten? I've brought some reference material, but we could hardly do that in a day or two."

Michael frowned. "There's always that possibility I suppose, but somehow I don't think it will happen. In fact . . ."

"What?"

"In fact, I think he made up his mind to let us shoot *before* last night."

"Before?"

"Yes. After I went home, I sat around thinking. Principally I was figuring how many bodies we can squeeze into those little rooms at the village inn, and what the bar tab will be. Then it suddenly struck me that Benson had given the okay right after I'd spoken to Sir Edmund. Nothing was really . . . how shall I put it? Mulled over. In retrospect it all seemed prearranged."

"If he was agreeable, why the standoff?"

"He was probably checking on the validity of the series. I'm sure Marchant's has agents in New York who could do that. It just took awhile—they're probably very thorough. All that time I was stewing for nothing and . . . hey . . . we're here."

We had almost passed two immense stone pillars to which iron gates were bracketed. We turned in. I saw that glossy black leaves adorned the gates in serpentine Gothic abundance. A small plaque attached to one read "Thorn Hill House."

"I almost missed it," Michael said.

Jittery, I peered ahead. "I thought we'd have more warning."

"You never see these houses from the road—they're always hidden by woods and by the contours of the land. It dips ahead, see?"

I did. We progressed to a little valley and the woods thinned. Giant tapered hedges—Irish yews—then lined the road, precisely spaced in regimental grandeur. We wound around another curve and the house hove into view. I managed not to gasp.

A great golden mass of Ham Hill stone, it sat three stories high in the middle of the vast meadow. Dozens of shining windows graced its Elizabethan symmetry, while a fantasy of detail kept the house from seeming stolid. Cylindrical chimneys rose beside curved gables, pediments and shell-like niches dotted the façade, odd carved beasts cringed in lofty alcoves, and oriels clung like limpets to both wings.

We drove into a courtyard flanked on either side by formal gardens. Balustraded pools adorned the velvet turf, and the courtyard walls were lichen grown. A filigreed orangery nestled to one side. As we pulled up, the house remained impassive. I had an overwhelming urge to giggle.

"There'll be a little note," I said. "No one at home today."

Michael swung an arm above my head to reach back for some luggage, and beneath the pitted Littell coat of arms, the massive door was opened. A rather stupefied butler emerged, blinking in the sunshine. In a strange parody of déjà vu, John Benson darted out behind him, dressed today in blazer and gray flannels.

"No trouble finding us, I see," he said. "Come in, come in."

We stepped through a passage, dim and cool, and then into an enormous hall. The floor beneath was stone and ancient beams hung far above. There were tapestries, Gobelins, I thought. Rows of ancestral portraits lined the walls, their subjects nestled dourly in the seamed and darkening oils. Benson led us up a broad stone staircase. On its ample landing sat a glass display case, incongruous there, which featured pairs of dueling pistols and rows of polished spurs arranged on a velvet-covered rod.

Benson made the obligatory speech of the country host. "You'll want to rest, of course. I've arranged for tea to be brought to your rooms. Drinks are at six in the billiard room."

I must have looked surprised because he added, "No one uses it for billiards any more, it's sort of an auxiliary parlor. Dinner is early here and dress is informal. Sir Edmund often arrives from London just in time to eat, and he prefers to keep things simple anyway." The thought of formal dinner dress had not occurred to me and Benson's dismissal of a trailing gown accented rather than eased my anxiety. What else had I overlooked?

The first-floor corridor stretched endlessly in both directions. Its carpet thickness and Hepplewhite appointments recalled my brief exposures to supremely *luxe* hotels. One-third down its length, I lost Michael.

"Your room is here, Mr. Grandville. Your luggage will be up in a moment," Benson said. "The house is large and we don't want you getting lost, so someone will come at six to show you to the billiard room."

All business, Michael thanked him and disappeared behind a door. We went on. At the end of the hallway stood a girl in a gray uniform, her hand on the doorknob, a trim little thing. Benson introduced us. "This is Sally. She'll look after you. Ring if you require anything," he waved airily. "Anything at all."

I went inside with Sally, jarred at the thought of her perched like a homing pigeon in some garret cage, waiting for my imperative buzz. Then I looked at her again. Her chestnut hair was brushed and shining, caught back in an almost soignée way. The uniform was nondescript but her shoes were burnished and beautifully made and—my eyes traveled upward—the face was just this side of saucy. If the male main chance walked through the manor door, Sally would be ready.

Woman to woman, she'd noticed my appraisal. I'd been sizing her up like a new student—the old schoolmistress trick. I blushed, but Sally turned and busied herself with the curtains. "There's a lovely view from these windows, miss."

There really was. I held the fold Sally had parted and gazed at the scene before me, entranced. The formal lawns extended a mile behind the house. They were the kind of green I'd never seen before today—the pure, keen, joyous green of the English landscape. At the lawn edges there were outbuildings, a lodge with an ogee roof, and a fringe of stables. Then the land rose into woods, dark trees whose tops moved almost imperceptibly in the breeze. A glint of water darted among them, the nip and shine of a little stream.

In a broad semicircle beyond, the village sat, squat stone and brick houses dozing in the afternoon sun, the square-towered parish church off to one side. Behind the village stood Thorn Hill, a nettled tor whose top was leveled, forming a little plateau. On the plateau a tent had been erected—a flapping, tatterdemalion, circuslike affair—shelter for the diggers who toiled up and down the slopes. The scene held a medieval enchantment—Sir Edmund's tiny, verdurous kingdom.

"This room is always light, miss," Sally said. "Years ago it was the nursery."

It must have been a happy place for children. Now the walls were yellow, the woodwork traced in bisque, its bright chintzes a perfect foil for the dark furniture. The bed was canopied and covered with a fringed linen spread which looked heavy enough to stand by itself. There was a knock at the door. A houseman entered with my bags.

"Shall I unpack for you, miss?"

"No thank you, Sally. I'll do that."

"Then I'll be back at six to take you to the billiard room."

"Yes, fine. That will be fine."

Sally went out and I felt relieved. She was so pert and I felt droopy, not up to making conversation. I also shied at the thought of her unpacking my things. What I'd brought seemed so utilitarian now—jerseys and slacks, two sweaters, two tweedy skirts, jeans for dirty work, a raincoat, and the ubiquitous navy blue dress—a skimpy assortment for this regal place. I found them depressing. They all but shouted out my image of myself: a faithfully functioning dronelike thing, practical to the point of tedium, without a glimmer of whimsey, grace, or—God forbid—glamour. I went to a mirror across the room and stared at myself. Did I look as dispirited as all that? The girl who looked back seemed anxious and prim, a wan reflection of someone who'd once had real involvement with life, who'd once been suffused with eagerness and—yes—passion.

I began halfheartedly unpacking, putting nightgowns in a drawer, hanging up my dress, setting out a few of my books. I came upon a printed scarf, lush with anemones and other flora, my one extravagance. I'd purchased it in an elegant Boston emporium the morning of my departure. It had been sinfully expensive, but I'd wanted something giddy and impractical, a girlish talisman to wear on my adventure. I placed it on the bureau top. Perhaps it would help a round-necked jersey and wool skirt pass for a dinner dress. Meanwhile, just looking at those riotous colors was a tonic of sorts.

Outside my window there was a sudden rush, a flurry, some agitated flapping, and a rasping screech. I went to see. A peacock whose erectile train was spread in green-gold glory was pursuing a peahen who was just then disappearing around the corner of the house. Two other peacocks followed after and the garden then regained its quiet.

The emerald lawns, the nodding flowers, the picture-book village—it all looked unreal. A pang went through me then—one I recognized as part panic, part longing for a more familiar setting. I felt desperately homesick for Langley, for my apartment and classroom, for the gently predictable pace of our daily events. I put my arms on the windowsill and my head upon my arms, feeling the warmth of the sunlight across my shoulders—but shivering still.

7

Edmund Littell came through the passageway, moved slowly into the room, and sat on a wooden bench.

He was alone. Others had been in this place and had seen what it held—but only because that had been necessary. They would not need to come again soon; perhaps he would see that they never came back. He rationed his own visits, held off for the days when the task seemed so hard—when the fine points of the plan made his head ache and the other men drove him to near despair. The students had a certain purity: it calmed him to consider their hard work and their loyalty. But the others—his noble lieutenants—his father would have refused to keep them as grooms.

He trusted no one but himself. That was the family imperative. His father and grandfather had been aloof in the same way—outwardly courteous, a sheath of reserve at the core. "Don't spend yourself on people beneath you," his grandfather said to him once. The old man thought him weak. He'd soon prove he was the strongest in that long chain of men who had lived on this land, serving England.

He rose from the bench and stepped up to a table. A square piece of baize covered the top. He lifted the cloth and raised the object that lay there, rubbing it gently with his thumb.

For a moment the room seemed to glow. He felt infused with a warmth *which restored his faith. He heard his dead father's voice, its timbre forbidding, and his own piping reply of the Tennyson lines ". . . thy name and glory cling/To all high places like a golden cloud/For ever . . ."*

In a few weeks the Return would be real—they would hold England, the jewel in the sea. When that happened each man would abide in the place God intended: those bred to it ruling, and the others obedient.

Honor would be restored. With the immigrants cast away, pure-blooded Englishmen would walk Britain's streets, run on her playing fields, father her children. The children would learn the new patriotism and grow up in innocence—corrupters would die with the filth they inspired.

He closed his eyes and saw the prow of a boat gliding out of the fens. The warrior it carried was not wounded, not dying—he sat erect and his breastplate gleamed in the mist.

Littell whispered. ". . . Then he drave/The heathen; after, slew the beast, and fell'd/The forest, letting in the sun, and made/Broad pathways for the hunter and the knight/And so return'd."

8

At six the clock on the village church began to chime and the sound was echoed through the house. My bedside table held a timepiece whose white enamel face was borne on the back of a brass elephant. As its hands slithered to the hour, the clock began to tinkle, the elephant's trunk gyrated creakily, and Sally tapped at my door. We went down without much conversation—I had the feeling she had other duties to nip back to.

The billiard room was too big to be cozy and the furniture in it was surprisingly sparse. There was no proper bar. A small trolley had been pressed into service, the bottles lined up on linen napkins covering its top. The bar tools looked square and masculine against the napkins' lacy fringes. I saw Michael talking to two men—one fair and tall, one slender and dark. Benson stood beside the trolley.

"May I offer you something, Miss Kendall? Sherry? Scotch? Fruit juice?"

"Juice would be nice, thank you."

"Mr. Grandville told me you had a good trip down."

"Yes. A fine trip. It went very quickly, really."

"It usually does. We're not *too* far from London. Sir Edmund is up and back several times a week. Ah, here's Dr. Trehane. How are you, Doctor?"

"Very well. Good of Edmund to ask me this evening. If that's really Scotch on the cart, I'd like to pry one out of you. I see you have found a charming young lady."

Trehane was a tanned seventy-plus and cheerily well preserved. Weather—the sun, wind, and sea—had etched deep lines in his face. His hair was white but his grip firm and his glance keen—almost boyish. He took my arm at once.

"You must be Miss Kendall. Your colleague Mr. Grandville just told me about your work with the film company. Your help must be invaluable."

"Well, I haven't really . . ."

"I hope you're not going to be modest, that's a total waste of time. Besides, I can tell you're able. You've a competent look about you."

"I assume that's a compliment, Dr. Trehane."

"It is. It is. And please call me Geoffrey. Makes me feel younger. Come sit down and tell me all about yourself."

We sat, and Trehane noticed my look around the nearly empty room.

"Surprised?"

"At what?"

"Surprised at the quiet evening?"

"It *is* a contrast to the London house."

"Oh, been to the other place, have you?"

"Last night."

"The London house is reserved for flossier entertainments. Here Edmund can be himself. Evenings at Thorn Hill have no frills at all."

"Perhaps he finds it a restful change."

"No such thing. Edmund's the hub and activity follows wherever he goes. For contemplative moments he takes a walk down the road. We have a little church in Thorn Hill . . ."

"Oh, yes. Michael described it to me."

"A most unusual little building. I'm very fond of it myself and Edmund dotes on it. I suppose he catches his few moments of repose there—it's a haven from the fray and when one is of a certain age, any haven is seductive. I've created a few of my own in recent years."

Geoffrey Trehane examined his drink for half a minute, then looked up again. "I'm retired now, my dear, from teaching history. After reciting that litany of people and places for so long it was hard to realize that I was part of the passing parade myself. However, there are compensations to retirement. Life has been far pleasanter than I expected, thanks to Edmund's generosity."

"Have you known each other long?"

"Long? All our lives, it seems. I . . ."

"Dr. Trehane." Benson was pointing to the door, where the butler signaled dinner was ready to be served.

"The drinking hours in this house are a sour joke," Trehane protested. "Well, I am bringing my Scotch along. We can talk at the table."

We drifted through the door to a long oak table in the dining hall. The host's chair was empty and Benson sat me to the right of it, with Michael opposite. Michael seemed perplexed, like an underwater swimmer who's emerged in some unfamiliar spot. I stared at him pointedly, but the look he returned was deliberately vacant. He introduced me to his two companions, Tom Marsden and Keith Gamble.

Gamble was tall and robust with thick yellow hair which had been tamed and smoothed across his head. Strong-jawed and cleft-chinned, he was a Cambridge graduate and former RAF captain who was the group leader—Michael explained—of the students conducting the dig. Slender, broody Marsden was Sir Edmund's new estate manager. The prototype of the taciturn Celt, he'd been at Thorn Hill just a week.

Michael's delivery, as always, was smooth. I got no clues to what was bothering him and anyway there was no time to glean them. Sir Edmund entered and sat down. All interest gravitated instantly to him. He discussed the film with Michael, a water pump with Marsden, and the weather with me. While he conversed his glance periodically slid down the table, where two places at its end were conspicuously empty.

Dr. Trehane stubbornly consumed his drink with his soup. When he had finished both, he turned to Sir Edmund. "I understand some farm implements have been found on the hill. That's a bit of luck."

Sir Edmund shook his head. "Implements may be too grand a term—they're fairly primitive. We've found what appear to be a plowshare, an axhead, and an awl. Gratifying, but hardly definitive."

"Dark Age, though, aren't they?"

"Well, very early, let's say." Sir Edmund looked at me. "These post-Roman digs are tricky. When the Roman influence disappeared, so did many of the solid crafts and the people turned to materials which were highly perishable—wood and leather, for instance, which simply disintegrated. There were no coins and hardly any inscriptions on the remaining pots to give us dates or clues. So there are few artifacts which provide us with an idea of the times."

"War tools, principally," I said, ". . . and farm tools."

"Exactly." Sir Edmund's tone was tinged with some embarrassment. "You must excuse me, Miss Kendall. I seem to be explaining by rote material which is wholly familiar to you."

"No . . . please. Please go on, Sir Edmund. Michael and I want to learn all we can about the dig." I glanced across the table and Michael nodded. "For the film, of course, but also for our own interest."

He was pleased. The tidy austerity of his expression softened then and his voice lifted. "Roman Britain was fairly prosperous. We have evidence of villas which had more than fifty rooms and well-to-do farmers who owned homes with central heating and window glass. When the Empire disintegrated, however, the towns were destroyed or left to rot, and the rural society withdrew into itself. Industry and technical expertise faded. Only the agricultural economy was left—and that conducted on a subsistence level in most areas. Perhaps in those times," Sir Edmund reflected, "men found comfort as well as sustenance in farming. With their world a shambles, they could at least depend on the constancy of the seasons and the rhythm of those ordinary tasks.

"Thorn Hill was intermittently farmed, although it was primarily used as a fort—its shape alone makes that obvious. We've found the usual complement of spears and knives but these are the first farming tools we've uncovered. If they do prove to be post-Roman it would be of great interest to us. We know so little about the daily lives of the Britishers," he added. "The Romans are well chronicled—they built in brick and stone. The pagan English—Angles and Saxons—left elaborate evidence in those sumptuous graves. It's the native British who are elusive. So you see, Mr. Grandville," Sir Edmund addressed himself to Michael, "we are constantly scrabbling for tidbits."

I saw Michael open his mouth to answer, then abruptly stop as his eyes shot to the door. I turned. Lily stood there, with David close behind. She was ashen, as before, and had dressed herself in layers of clothing—a long, dark skirt, creamy blouse, embroidered vest, and knitted shawl. At her breast, slender fingers splayed protectively over the shawl knot, as if the clothing provided emotional insulation as well as warmth.

Her voice was high pitched, cutting. "Still touting your precious fossils, Father? I'm grateful you've found a new audience."

Sir Edmund rose, startled. "Felicia," he said, "I was worried. Were you delayed?"

"No. Just dithering as usual."

I thought he'd rebuke her, but he just looked confused.

"My dear," he asked, "are you feeling well?"

"I'm fine, Father . . . just fine." She and David moved to the table's end. "If my timing is correct, I've missed one bowl of soup and the opening segment of the weekly lecture. Can't say I feel deprived. Do you, David?"

"What?"

"Do you feel deprived?"

"That's enough, Lily," David answered. "Behave yourself."

She stopped then, and we all fell silent. Benson made some rabbity gestures over his rolls, tearing them into little pieces, while Michael studiously rearranged his silver. I found I could neither look at Sir Edmund, nor dredge up any plausible ice-breaker. Dr. Trehane then blessedly performed that function.

"I understand the rest of your people are due here Monday, Mr. Grandville."

"That's right. Our director, the technicians, and the writer. Which reminds me, Sir Edmund, I'd like to discuss the script with you, if I may."

"Yes, of course," Littell said. "Give it to me after dinner. I'll read it and we can talk in the morning. Will you be filming directly on the hill?"

"On it and all around it. We'll be very careful not to interfere with the excavations. As for the script, I'm pretty sure it's factually correct, but it may be heavy with local legends. Perhaps you can advise us which we should emphasize and which would be better played down."

"Tell me, Grandville," Keith Gamble said, "are these legends Dark Age?"

"Largely, yes."

"Specifically, are they Arthurian?"

"Yes."

"What are you getting at, Keith?" asked Dr. Trehane.

"Well," Gamble lounged back in his chair and smiled derisively, "film crews have a way of attracting attention and we could have the press down here in no time. Anything that smacks of Arthur gets pasted on the front pages. We'll have tour busloads of people clamoring for verified ashes and cheap teas."

I'd never seen Michael so angry. He kept his voice down but his look was lethal. "Perhaps you've not been exposed to a modern film crew before, Mr. Gamble. We're not Metro-Goldwyn-Mayer you know, moving hundreds of people about. We're simply a handful of professionals interested in doing the job and usually too tired at the end of the day to stand around running off at the mouth."

"That may be," Gamble persisted, "but I've found a little pub-talk goes a long way. The villagers are canny enough to know that legends mean customers."

"Surely the villagers realize the import of the dig. What do they think the students are doing—catching butterflies?"

Gamble's laugh was bark-sharp and humorless. "Very amusing, Grandville, but the fact is that we've managed to keep a low profile down here. Since the effort is privately funded, there's little public involvement. We . . ."

"Keith," Sir Edmund interrupted, "I think we may assume that Mr. Grandville and his associates will be prudent." He turned to Michael. "Perhaps you can keep the legendary aspects pared to a minimum. After all, we've just a modest fund of information on the subject . . . most of it supposition. I don't think you'd want the film indulging in speculation."

"No. Of course not."

"Then we understand each other. Some day . . . ," Sir Edmund paused, ". . . some day we may have more pieces of the puzzle and can portray Arthur as he really was."

"As he *really* was, Father," Lily shrilled from the table's end.

"A Romano-British thug in a leather kilt."

The pain which flickered across Sir Edmund's face was so palpable that it made me flinch. He stared at Lily blankly, as if she were some creature he had never seen before. When he finally spoke, his voice had the slightest rasp, as if his mouth had gone quite dry. He cleared his throat, then said: "When Arthur was young there were elderly men about who had been born and educated in a world still Roman. They had enjoyed a fine and stable civilization . . . then watched its destruction . . . but lacked the strength to act in some decisive way. Arthur entered that void and struggled for two decades to preserve justice and order.

"The way we measure men is not by what they do in their own lifetime, but what they pass along to their successors. Legends about Arthur have not persisted by accident. They live because he created an age which is the foundation of British history. He gave us our tenacity, our spirit, and our morality. Above all, he gave us a vision of Britain as it ought to be." Sir Edmund rose and gestured towards his plate. "I believe I'm finished with my dinner. Please excuse me." Without another word, he left.

I counted the steps he took to remove himself from the room. Fourteen, exactly. We then became two rows of fork-pushers, rearranging food but eating very little. Solemn Marsden, oddly, was the first to speak. "I've some business to attend to," he said brusquely, walking out. Benson mumbled something about obligations of his own and left. Gamble patted his tie, bowed briefly in my direction, made a deeper bow to Lily, and sauntered off.

With her father gone, Lily seemed deflated. The rod of spite which held her upright had been whisked away and she looked pinched and miserable. Dr. Trehane walked around the table and sat next to her, talking softly. Michael's head inclined toward the door. We stood and said our good-nights quickly.

In the hall, he fumed. "Contentious little bitch! Why did she have to stage a scene tonight?"

"She's disturbed, Michael. Upset."

"Upset, is she? I'd like to upend her over my knee and give her the paddling of her life. It might be the most constructive action anyone's taken toward her." He made a fist and slammed it into the palm of his other hand. "My God, what a can of worms! All I wanted was a few days' quiet shooting. How can I approach Sir Edmund with the script tonight? What do you think, Beth? Wouldn't business-as-usual seem too callous?"

"Michael," I touched his arm and tried to sound soothing, "perhaps he'd think it more peculiar if you didn't submit the script. Proceeding as usual might make less of the incident, somehow."

"You may be right. I suppose I should take my cue from Littell and develop some stiff upper lip. That might see me through. Except . . . "

"What, Michael?"

"Except that *nothing* feels right here. With all the sturdy entrepreneurs in Britain, I have to pick one with a batty daughter and a hallowed dig."

"Please, won't you take it a step at a time? Bring the script up to Sir Edmund now and see what happens. The rest may be smooth sailing."

He smiled. "Tell me, why are plays written about nymphs and harridans instead of the calm and sensible women of this world?"

"Because they're much too dull. Go on now."

"What will you do?"

"I'll have a bath and read, then go to sleep."

He hesitated, troubled. "I feel I'm neglecting you."

"Don't be silly. It's been a long day, anyhow."

His face cleared. "Yes, it has. A long day. All right then, Beth. Good night."

We parted and with some mental calculations I found the right stairway, the right corridor, and the right room. My bed had been turned down and the sheets felt as though they'd been loomed in heaven. A little book had been placed on the bedside table. Poems.

The bath was a somber Victorian shrine encased in mahogany and at least eight feet long. There was a bunch of autumn gentian on the marble washstand, though, warmed towels on the towel bar, and a bottle of scented bath crystals on the shelf near the basin. I bathed in steamy elegance, then—wrapped in toweling—padded out to get a nightgown.

I opened the drawer and my fingers flicked past jeans and sweaters to some pastel underthings. My eye just caught a sliver of brightness at the bottom of the stack, and I pushed the lingerie aside. There, neatly folded, lay my botanical scarf, the one I had left on the bureau-top before going downstairs. I stared down at it, dumbfounded. How had it gotten there?

Uneasy, I crossed to the desk to examine my purse. Money, passport, traveler's checks were all intact. My writing case lay open as I'd left it, receipts and stamps in their proper compartments, the writing pad smooth and white. Smooth. I ran my fingertips along its surface. Before leaving London, I'd made notes on the pad, thoughts on the filming which I'd given to Michael. The notes had been made on the thin writing paper with a ballpoint pen, but the pad's top sheet now carried no impression of the memo. Someone had removed it. Someone had lifted that pile of underthings to the bureau top while they went through the drawer and inadvertently picked up the scarf when they replaced them. Systematically and quite thoroughly, someone had been searching my room.

I sat down, fury and queasiness combatant inside me. The thought that this house harbored someone bloodless enough to paw through my intimate clothing was hard to absorb. I found it repellent. Even at Langley, where the staff lived side by side in a community of interwoven relationships, privacy was sacred. In a queer, disturbing way, I felt violated.

What to do? If all had gone well, Michael would now be closeted with Sir Edmund. I could predict Benson's response to my call: bland platitudes masking a conviction that I was overtired and overimaginative. Sally would have to be approached with tact or she might think I was accusing her. Somehow I hadn't the strength for that conversation now.

Tomorrow. The morning would bring sunshine and clarity. I'd be rested and able to cope. I crossed to my door and turned its lock, slipped into a nightgown, got into bed, and picked up the book of poems. They were Early English—sober, epic, eloquent. I had no doubt they had been put there at Sir Edmund's direction.

I read through a translation of *The Ruin*, a description of a deserted Roman city, caught as always by the haunting last paragraph.

> "Came days of pestilence, on all sides men fell dead,
> death fetched the flower of the people;
> where they stood to fight, waste places
> and on the acropolis, ruins."

Pestilence, waste places, ruins. A poignant ending to my day. I turned off the light and lay back, thinking. With thievery ruled out, why would anyone search my room? What could I possibly have in my possession that someone else would want to see? Then a chilling thought—would they be back? I tossed, turning from side to side as I always did in strange beds, pulling at covers, plucking at pillows, restless, edgy, worried. I remember the wind coming up and the trees stirring, the creak and tinkle of the little clock and then—nothing.

9

Littell walked up to the lodge with Gamble, who carried a pocket flash just strong enough to light the path. The lodge interior was as bare and functional as a seminary basement; the students present rose as they came through the door.

Sir Edmund nodded and they sat down. He studied the group for a moment, then said, "Because you've been selected for this work, I wanted to see you myself. The success of the project depends on your nerve and judgment.

"What you must do will be dangerous, but you'll have the means of protecting yourselves. Use your equipment carefully and you will all come through in good health.

"Remember our movement is based on three principles—planning, training, and purpose. The plan has been constructed so that it cannot fail. Your training has been the best. Our purpose and duty are clear . . . to create not just a new government, but a new age. What you do in the next few weeks will mark England for hundreds of years."

As he turned to leave, a large blond boy raised his hand.

"Yes?"

"Sir, we've heard rumors . . . Thorn Hill isn't the only camp, is it? Are there other men in the North?"

*"*Just *a minute . . . ," Gamble objected.*

"Let him be," Sir Edmund said. "We do have men in the North and throughout England. Not a gigantic force, perhaps, but then we've other means at our command.

"What you're asking is . . . is this force sufficient? I tell you now, it is. I would have preferred to fight this battle with reason and persuasion . . . but that's not to be. We'll win with strategy and military skills.

"And weapons," he added softly. "Weapons they've not seen before."

On the flash-lit path Sir Edmund asked, "Who is that boy?"

"Philip Atherton."

"What school?"

"Sandhurst," Gamble answered.

"Who picked him?"

Gamble hesitated. "I did. He shouldn't have asked . . ."

"Never mind. He'll do."

You picked him, Sir Edmund thought, because he looks like you. Because he reminds you of what you were at twenty-one. But you never had that drive. Remembering Atherton's clear, uncompromising stare, Littell decided: that one is made of steel.

10

I was awakened by a gentle tapping and, when I had roused myself sufficiently to stand upright, saw a white envelope had been slipped beneath the door. It was a telephone message transcribed in fine, old-fashioned script: Dr. Trehane would like to take me on a tour of Thorn Hill, he'd stop by about ten. I walked to the window. There was no sunshine after all. It was a raw, gray day, and the village—underneath the clouds—seemed carved in pumice. I dressed quickly and went downstairs.

The billiard room looked cheerier in daylight. A fire crackled in the enormous grate and small tables had been set around the room, each covered in white linen and equipped with a tiny bell. A ring of the bell produced a maid bearing a formidable breakfast—juice, steaming porridge, coddled eggs, sausage, buttered toast, thick-cut, grapefruit marmalade, and coffee. I surprised myself by sampling everything, then remembered I'd just picked at last night's dinner. When the maid returned with a pot of fresh coffee, I asked after Mr. Grandville.

"He went out early this morning, miss, with Mr. Gamble. They went up the hill."

Reconnoitering and choosing camera positions, I thought.

Well and good, except that Michael would probably have preferred to do his scouting alone. I was in the front hall pulling on my coat when Trehane arrived, looking ruddier than ever. "Dress warmly, Elizabeth," he said. "It's a chilly day."

His car was an ancient, piebald Austin revved up—Trehane assured me—in my honor. "Not that I doubt your endurance, my dear, but it's a half-hour walk just to clear the grounds."

At nearly midday there was no hustle in the village. The streets were sedate and still, as if all vitality had drained off to the manor at one end, to Thorn Hill at the other. We parked and walked past the shops until there was turf underfoot and the ragged paths which led up the hill came into view. It was a surprisingly steep climb which Trehane made easily, holding my arm while I floundered and scrabbled for branches and tussocks. At the top there was no even plateau but about fifteen acres of undulating ground, pocked with several excavations in varying forms of development. I could see the students crouched in the earth or pushing wheelbarrows and—at the end of the field—Michael and Keith Gamble walking the perimeter. The tent, which seemed somewhat festive from below, sagged in soiled accordion folds. Inside it, a scarred metal table held a hotplate and a kettle, some chipped cups, and a dish of teabags. Old wooden chairs sat rather tipsily on the earthen floor.

"Well," Trehane said, "to do this work you've got to tolerate the camping-out aspects. I'm all for creature comforts myself."

"How long have they been doing this?"

"It varies, Elizabeth. Some of the boys stay six months or so, but there are at least a dozen who've been with it from the beginning—at least two years."

"They must be unusually dedicated."

"Edmund seems to infuse them with an odd *esprit*. Odd, because he's very seldom up here. It's just that they know he's totally dedicated to uncovering our national origins—the purely

British beginnings. It inspires them, I suppose. It *must*—to have them scrounging in the dirt all day." He laughed. "As you can see, I'm most appreciative of archeological finds when they're fully discovered and neatly dusted off. A typical armchair dilettante."

We watched one boy cast about with a banjo-shaped instrument. A soil conductivity meter, Trehane said. "Works on the same principle as radar, pointing up subsurface features such as postholes. Postholes are important because they may give clues to post-Roman ramparts. So far the group has discovered traces of Neolithic and Pre-Roman Iron Age settlements, but nothing that's conclusively Dark Age. It's discouraging."

"They don't appear to be discouraged." I watched the workers plodding methodically about. In spite of the gray day and grubby work, they seemed engrossed.

"Youth, my dear Elizabeth. It more readily absorbs the slings and arrows—*and* the aching backs."

I looked across the field again. Michael and Keith had disappeared over the hill. A disappointment. I knew I could not discuss my intruder in Keith's presence, but just speaking to Michael for a moment would have been a comfort.

". . . no great discoveries today," Trehane said.

"What? I'm sorry, Geoffrey. I was distracted for the moment."

"I was just saying that it seems a fairly routine morning here. Shall we go down?"

I virtually slid down the hill, flailing for support again. At bottom I glanced at my hands. They looked like those of a grubby schoolchild and I stuffed them in my pockets. "I'd hate to make that trip in the dark."

"People do," Trehane said. "Not the staff, of course. They're properly wary of falling into pits. But the natives hereabouts have crept up more than once."

"Good heavens, what for?"

"If there's the slightest whiff of gossip about the day's find, some locals with dreams of treasure will make the climb at night. They bring hoes and shovels, you know, and that's disastrous."

"You mean they *dig?*"

"That and other things. Stumble and trample is what they seem to do best. There was a nasty episode here last spring. The team had unearthed a cache of pottery—interesting rim-sherds, mostly—and were sifting the cache area for further finds. I guess one of the boys was filled with enthusiasm—it's hard to be cool when something turns up—and he mentioned it in the village. The next morning the pottery was ground to dust and the sifted area so trampled that the team had to begin digging again. They figured it took five or six men to do that much damage. The boys were really upset."

"That's awful."

"It's never pleasant to be confronted with raw greed of that magnitude," Trehane said, shaking his head, "but it exists, Elizabeth, it exists."

We walked slowly back to the village with Trehane pointing out the cottages of friends. "My own is over there," he said, waving his stick. "It's not mine, really. Edmund leases it to me for a piddling sum, so I've enough left over for my needs and for Mrs. Tierney, who knows how to look after old bachelors. Snug. It's a snug arrangement. I hoped I'd drop into some such niche when I retired—the fact that it's such a downy one I owe to Edmund." His smile faded. "Poor Edmund. It's ironic that my life has been relatively contented and his so unhappy."

"You said you've been his friend for a very long time."

"Instructor and then friend. I was just down from Oxford when I was engaged to be his tutor. Edmund had a bout with rheumatic fever as a boy and had to leave school for a while. I was hired to bridge the gap and I enjoyed it. He was a bright student—responsive, imaginative—a brilliant boy, really."

I thought of Marchant's and its multiple affiliates, hundreds of pinheads on a map of the world. "It's a shame that imagination was boxed into a career which is so . . . practical."

"But business is no dungeon for him. He gets real satisfaction from his work and his career has kept him from floundering several times in his life. When Margaret died, for instance."

"She was very young, wasn't she?"

"Pitifully young," Trehane shook his head. "Made for each other is a trite phrase, but those two surely were. Margaret adored him and for Edmund, Margaret was *life.* He was much older, and he'd been through a lot in the war. When he got back to Thorn Hill his own father was dying and he totally immersed himself in taking over the estate. Became a kind of monk, actually. Then Margaret came on the scene and he began to live again. She saved him from a kind of isolation which could have become a morbid habit. Edmund never really got over Margaret's death and Felicia hasn't been much of a comfort."

There seemed no delicate way to phrase the question, so I put it bluntly. "Why is she so angry?"

Trehane looked straight at me, startled. "Strange you should use that term. Angry is precisely the word I've been thinking of since Felicia's scene last night. She never was angry before. Obstinate, yes. Occasionally petulant. But I've never heard her speak so hatefully to her father. Poor child. I can't imagine what's come over her."

We had reached a river, sedate and peaceful, bounded by hanging boughs and shafts of prickly teasel. A stone bridge with medieval arches stretched across it and the road beyond led to a solid, gray-gold fourteenth-century church. High up in its nave, plump burgher-donors were limned in stained glass, alternating with Saint George and John the Baptist.

"What a lovely church!" I marveled, and pointing to the civilians in the windows, asked, "Were they early Littells?"

"I don't know," Trehane was amused, "but I'm sure they were surprised to find themselves in togas. I've never understood why flowing garments imply purity of soul. But *wait*—the surprise—the mother church—is up the road."

We walked beyond the churchyard into a little lane. Trehane led the way, primed with anticipation. "Just past this grove," he said, taking my arm again. "There!"

The building was tiny—twenty-five by twelve or thirteen feet perhaps. Its stones had the rubbed and powdery look most ancient buildings share. Two reeded pilasters framed the rounded door and narrow windows were chiseled out of nave and chancel. A church. A church which had stood before Ethelred and Alfred, when tribal wars raged through these fields and valleys and Britain still languished in darkness. I found I'd instinctively caught my breath.

Trehane was watching me closely.

"Eighth century?" I asked.

"Seventh. It was unrecognized for years, unused and hemmed in by other buildings. In the 1700s a farmer built a chimney stack into it and tenants used it as a cottage. It's called the Skull House in the old deeds, so we think that during the Middle Ages it was used as a charnel house. The stone outbuildings are medieval," he said, pointing to two behind the church.

"Who found it then?"

"Edmund's grandfather, William Littell. In 1915, during some alterations, a pair of stone angels were discovered. They were built into a wall, which piqued Sir William's interest and he began a program of research and restoration. Edmund has had experts in ancient stonework here—one chap came from Lebanon a few years ago. He confirmed signs of early Saxon tool marks in the working of the stones. Would you like to see inside? I have a key." He fished it from his pocket and inserted it in the oaken door.

The interior seemed infinitely touching—rough, poor, and totally plain—save for the dangling iron chandeliers and a basket of dried field flowers placed near the wooden altar. The twin stone angels flew above the chancel arch, their halos skewed and feet aloft in skittish, primitive caricature. I tried to visualize an early congregation.

"It's hard for me to conceive of British Christianity going this far back, Geoffrey. Druids and Roman gods and pagan rites . . . but not this."

"Shadowy . . . the origins of the faith in England are shadowy at best," Trehane responded. "We do know that Christianity must have been established in Britain by the fourth century . . . there were several British bishops at the Council of Arles in 314 and the Council of Rimini in 359. And then, of course, there's evidence that Arthur himself was a Christian. The Easter annals refer to the battle of Badon as one at which 'Arthur carried the cross of Our Lord Jesus Christ on his shoulders for three days and three nights and the Britons were victors.' "

"A Herculean feat."

"Indeed," Trehane agreed, "and perhaps it never happened, but it's part of the legend . . . a legend which is as potent today as it was in the Middle Ages."

"Really?"

"Yes, Elizabeth. In bad times people look for saviors. The Return of Arthur seems to have captured the modern imagination. Seminars are cropping up at universities, bolstered by the literature and by Dark Age archeology. I've met some otherwise sophisticated people who believe that Arthur will be back . . . in one form or another . . . to lead Britain to a golden age."

"Are they serious?"

"More serious than they'll admit . . . even to themselves. Arthur is part of Britain's fabric, after all. His exploits are our legacy, and his Return the essential British myth." He smiled. "A psychiatrist would tell you that a man approaching the end of his own life will often fuse a longing for rebirth and renewal with some legendary figure. I've had some stirrings like that myself."

"Geoffrey . . ."

"All firmly resisted, of course. *So,*" he straightened up and looked around, "seventh-century Britain was an ecclesiastical stew, my dear . . . some Druid cults still intoning in the woods, Celtic paganism flourishing elsewhere, the remains of Roman temples dotting the countryside, monasteries growing in number, and churches like this," he turned to view the chamber, "to serve the few faithful in this area."

I stood there, stirred at the thought of men who—centuries ago—foresook superstition and a jumble of deities to kneel on these stone floors. "It seems," I said to Geoffrey, "a very special place. Does it affect you the same way? Move you, that is?"

"It does," he answered. "Every time I step through the door. It's only myself and Edmund who come with any regularity, you see. This is really a family chapel and few others are allowed—the occasional scholar perhaps. Edmund's terribly protective about the church. I think it means more to him than the manor or the village—or even Thorn Hill. I've often come upon him sitting alone. Even a half-hour here seems to refresh his spirit."

I wondered how Geoffrey Trehane behaved in those instances. Would there be the discreet cough, the shuffled foot to signal his presence? No. More likely he would tiptoe backwards and leave his friend and benefactor in unsullied peace.

Privilege. The word hadn't held much reality for me before. The Langley students who summered on yachts in the Aegean and took the winter holidays at Klosters had simply seemed unpolished girls. But the deference—indeed reverence—accorded Edmund Littell through his lifetime struck me now. Finely bred, born to riches, earning more—he could command loyalty on those strengths alone. His people had a deeper reason for affection, though. They must love him because he could be humbled by this little place.

It was after one when Geoffrey dropped me back at the house. I went up to my room and found a bowl of fruit on the desk, each gleaming piece hand polished. There was a china plate beside the bowl and an ivory-handled paring knife. I picked up the apple gratefully—better to eat here than run the luncheon gantlet—and decided to choose some clothes for dinner. It would take time to rearrange the meager ingredients into something presentable, then I'd have the crumbs of security gleaned from knowing I'd done my best. I had the lot laid out on the bed and was eyeing it dubiously when there was a knock at the door and Sally looked in.

"Am I intruding, miss? Mr. Grandville asked me to give you this envelope." She saw the apple. "Are you hungry? Would you like a tray?"

"No thanks. Come in Sally, will you? I need advice."

"From me, miss?" Sally's laugh was buoyant.

"In this department I'm sure you're expert. Oops!" The envelope was large and slippery—and held our script. I skimmed some pages. Judging by the detail in it, I'd have several hours' work to do. "Is Mr. Grandville here now?"

"No, miss," Sally answered. "He went off again with Mr. Gamble. He told me to tell you he'd see you this evening."

"Oh?" That sounded somewhat peremptory, but messages often seemed abrupt. "Well, sit down please Sally. I'm trying to fix up something to wear tonight—I'm afraid I've brought too little clothing."

"I wouldn't fret about it, miss. If you'll not think me rude for saying so, you could come down in a gunnysack for all this group would notice." Sally's cheeks had turned quite pink.

"Group? What group?" I teased.

"The gentlemen, miss. Mr. Benson thinks only of Sir Edmund, and Mr. Gamble of the dig on the hill. Mr. Marsden doesn't speak to anyone. I've said good-morning to him at least four times and gotten silence for my trouble. To be truthful, the whole village is a dead loss socially."

Spirited, her eyes bright, Sally looked prettier than ever. I'd be annoyed too, I thought—annoyed and worried if I thought my youth was being wasted here.

"Are there no local boys . . ."

"Clods," Sally pronounced.

"And the students?"

"Them?" Sally's tone was scathing. "Snobbish. They live off at the lodge and keep to themselves. I don't think they'd look at a girl without money or title." She sat straight up in her chair. "I'm saving to go to school in London. I've almost enough put away."

"To the univerity?"

"No, miss." Sally discarded academia without a qualm. "I'll be a secretary. Training like that no one can take away from you."

Indeed not, I thought, and Sally would make the most of it. I had another question for her now.

"Sally," I began hesitantly, knowing I'd have to couch it in the most delicate terms. "Last night—when I went down to dinner—did you come back here to straighten up my clothes?"

"Your clothes?" Sally looked surprised. "No, miss. You told me you preferred to unpack yourself. I came up to turn down your bed and leave the little book."

"The poems?"

"Poems, were they? I found them in your cubby . . ."

I held up my hand. "What cubby?"

"Downstairs there is a wall of cubbies, Miss Kendall. Off the pantry. Like the shelves in the library, you see, but partitioned. One cubby for each bedroom and double-size for the ground-floor rooms. Several times a day the maids are supposed to check the cubbies of the rooms they're responsible for. Some guests may have asked for a particular type of pillow or need extra linen—and the housekeeper puts it in the proper cubbyhole. Or the guest may have admired a particular flower outside. In that case there'd be a vase of the right size with a note tucked inside it for the gardener. I'd go to him, get the bouquet, put it in the vase and put the vase in the room. Things like that."

Evidently Thorn Hill House ran like a well-oiled machine. I thought the housekeeper must be a paragon of efficiency.

"And you didn't rearrange my bureau-top or start to lay out a nightgown?"

"No, miss." Sally was beginning to look anxious. "Is there something you can't find?"

"No, Sally, no. Please," I patted her arm, "put that out of your mind. When I came back upstairs some of my belongings seemed to be in different places, but I could have moved them myself and forgotten."

She stood up, stiff and a little unsure. "If there's nothing else, I'll go now. Miss Felicia plans to spend the week, so I've a lot to do."

"Of course—and Sally, thank you for everything." I hoped my smile conveyed both warmth and apology for the questions. She did relax a bit and we walked to the door together.

"I suppose when Felicia's here the house is in a whirl."

"Yes, she surely stirs things up," Sally agreed, "but we get along. We played together . . . you know . . . when we were children."

"A sad childhood she must have had, with her mother gone."

"Sad?" Sally looked mildly astonished. "No, miss. Never sad. She was the happiest child I've ever known."

11

I came down that evening to find Michael and David in deep conversation at the trolley bar, their drinks set down and ignored, their faces somber.

"Hi."

David jumped, then—seeing me—relaxed. "Hello, Elizabeth. I thought you were Lily."

"If that's the effect she has on you, I don't think you've much of a future together."

"I'm feeling depressed. Join the circle and we'll tell you why."

"David's been speaking to London today," Michael began.

"To some friends on newspapers up there," David said. "Apparently the police don't have a single lead on Jock's murder."

"Not yet?"

"They're flummoxed. Embarrassed, as a matter of fact. Jock's manager arrived so soon after the deed that the police thought they had a good start. But nothing's materialized. It was one of those clean jobs . . . too clean for a thief or an amateur seeking revenge."

"You mean he was killed by a professional?"

"Perhaps not by someone who made a career of it, but certainly someone who'd murdered before."

"That's horrible."

"The police think so too. They're still at square one. More to the point," David continued, "we think Lily may be in for some serious questioning."

"But . . . as Michael said . . . she was at home all day."

"Yes, that's easily established. But I imagine they'd want to plumb the depths of Lily's knowledge of Jock's friends . . . with so few clues they'll be scraping the barrel. I should add that we're not sharing this information with Lily just now."

"Is that wise? Shouldn't she be prepared?"

"We think it's best," Michael answered. "Lily's shaken enough by Jock's death without hearing the gruesome details and worrying about being further involved."

"All right," I said, subdued. "I won't say anything."

Precisely on cue, Lily came through the double doors. She was smiling—an incandescent smile which altered her appearance remarkably. She went directly to Michael, placed her fingertips on his lapel, and fluttered. The words were commonplace enough, but the message was pure maiden-in-distress or, in Lily's extravagant style, the hummingbird-impaled. I heard her murmur, "You'll help me do that, won't you?"

"I haven't acted in a long time, Lily," Michael demurred, "and teaching was never one of my strong points."

"Darling, I'm just asking you to *listen* to me. I'm sure you can give me a few words of advice."

"All right, I'll try," Michael glanced at David, who stood there stiff faced. Lily caught the look which passed between them and I saw her mouth twitch. She leaned instantly toward David.

"Father won't be dining downstairs this evening. Isn't that nice, darling? No history lessons. No dull talk. Just you and I having a quiet time together." She wove her arm through his and they walked off.

"Remarkable," Michael said after a moment. "I don't know why she thinks she needs instruction. Her natural talents exceed any acting tips I could offer."

"David has so much patience with her."

"It's a form of desperation. Hey!" He put his hand under my chin and tilted my face up toward his. "You're looking woeful. Have a hard day?"

"Not a bad day but a spooky night," I managed to answer equably. Then I told him about my intruder. When I finished he was frowning.

"I don't know what's going on, but I can tell you I don't like it. If someone wants to see our credentials, why don't they just ask?"

"Your room wasn't searched?"

"It could have been and I didn't notice. Too preoccupied . . . or tense."

"Oh? I saw you tramping the hill with Gamble and I thought things were going well."

"Well enough, Beth. We have to shoot the sequence within fairly strict boundaries. Not quite what I hoped for, but adequate, I guess. And Gamble's attitude was helpful enough, an improvement over last night anyway."

"Look, Michael, he may have reason to be protective." I reported Trehane's tale of the midnight vandals.

"Hmm." Michael sounded doubtful. "Somehow I can't see Gamble as the champion of archeology. He's no scholar, that's for sure. I think all that raving at the table was bluster to cover up his lightweight abilities. Directing the dig must be a cushy job and I guess he hopes to keep it as long as he can."

"Sounds reasonable," I sighed and looked away.

"That was quite a sigh."

"I'm restless Michael. I'd like to . . . to get on with whatever contribution I can make and . . ."

"And be finished?" Michael asked.

"Working will make the week go faster," I added lamely. "I *do* feel I'm here under false pretenses and work is my usual antidote for insecurity."

"Then work you shall have," Michael pulled roughly at his tie knot and ran both hands through his hair. "Meanwhile," he said briskly, "shall we have dinner?"

I could hardly miss the stony undertones. They provoked the obligatory pang of guilt, then—for the first time—a surge of anger. Why did I feel I had to please Michael at any cost to my common sense and self-esteem? Why couldn't the "good little girl" in me be soothed, then buried—preferably in some pit reserved for witless ingenues? I let Michael take my arm and forced a smile, but inside the terms of reckoning were churning. I'd do the job—such as it was—and get back to London quickly.

Dinner was a self-help buffet, rather sparsely attended. Neither Sir Edmund nor Benson appeared; their "regrets" explained they were working. Gamble and Marsden came and went, observing the barest amenities, and Lily and David seemed oblivious to us all. After the meal, Geoffrey Trehane "popped" in—quite literally so—since his gray head and burnished outdoor smile appeared around the door, then his whole tweedy self. His arms were laden with books and papers, one or two dribbling down onto the carpet. I retrieved these while Michael eased the bulk of his burden onto a table.

"Thank you. Thanks so much, old man," Trehane dropped into a chair. "There can't be anything heavier than a pile of books. Deadweight but lively thoughts, eh?" He paused to catch his breath. "I've just had ten minutes with Edmund. I needed his ideas on this pamphlet I'm doing on the church and village." He laughed. "Subtitled: Who knifed who through the ages."

"A historical pamphlet?" I asked.

"Oh, primarily, with the usual cultural and architectural details. I spent a week last month at the Bodleian—that noble labyrinth—fiddling with twelfth-century manuscripts and Middle English. Edmund's little press here will publish the finished product. My bid for immortality." He looked discomfited. "The trouble about delving into the stacks again is that it reminds you of all the lost opportunities for genuine scholarship. Lost or wasted. Reminds one of so much time—so much breath—squandered on idle chatter."

"Geoffrey," I tapped his arm and he looked over at me. "I'll really look forward to your pamphlet. I can't think of a more fascinating subject."

"Thank you, my dear," he answered, and glanced about absently. He's tired, I thought, and this was verified by the weary way he hauled himself out of the chair again.

"I must be off. Lots of work still to do tonight."

"Do you need a lift?" Michael asked.

"Thanks, no. I have a car outside."

"I'll give you a hand." I picked up a briefcase and one stack of books. "Be back in a minute, Michael."

In the hall, I suggested to Geoffrey that he cut back a bit. "There's no deadline, is there? Can't you take it at an easier pace. Rest more?"

Trehane chucked his coat over his arm and turned to face me. "There's a saying hereabouts . . . 'plenty of rest in the grave.' "

I must have grimaced, for he added quickly, "Forgive an old man who's feeling his age tonight."

He brightened just a bit. "The job's really absorbing, you know. I keep tripping over myths and legends and there's also what I call the old codger school of history . . . the stories our crusty ancients pass along. A local favorite is the tale of a great treasure found here fifty years ago."

"Thorn Hill seems too quiet for a treasure trove."

"I agree, but when a story persists long after the principals have departed, I'm inclined to believe there's some truth involved."

I stood outside the car while Geoffrey set his books in the back and—after we said goodbye—watched the lights of the Austin weave down the drive. I was thinking of Miss Langley and the kinship she and Geoffrey shared—the habit of grace in adversity. They were the last survivors of another world. A better world, I decided, as I turned back to the house. Inside I saw Michael was still seated at the study table. I called good-night and kept on walking. I was tired, and a reprise of the shooting schedule was more than I cared to face.

My room, at least, was a comfort. Someone had started a little fire and it flickered on the solid furnishings, the brasswork, the old pictures in old frames. I lay down on a *vert 'anglais* chaise, book in hand, read until I slept, then woke chilled and rumpled. The fire had gone out and my book was on the floor. The clock said half-past two. I groaned. With five hours of deep sleep behind me, falling off again would be impossible. The room was cold and—when I slipped my hand beneath the covers—the bed seemed even colder. I crossed to the window seat where the extra covers were stored and felt among them in the shadows—sturdy English blankets and a drift of mohair. I pulled the mohair out, put down the lid, and was about to turn—when a movement in the garden below just caught my eye.

What lay beneath my window was a rectangle of lawn, bordered by yews and roses and quartered by gravel paths which met in the center at a balustraded pool. It was at the edge of this rectangle where the foliage moved. As I watched, transfixed, a figure detached itself from the hedges and stepped onto the open lawn. I sprinted back across the room, snapped off my little bedlamp and ran to the window again. Illuminated by the moon and its pearly nimbus, three figures now stood in the open. Slowly—in some secretive pavane—they began to move across the lawn.

They were carrying something. Parcels. Wrapped parcels in long, narrow shapes. "Hoes and shovels, my dear," Geoffrey had said. "They dig."

Bonded to the window in fear-tinged disbelief, I saw them cross the garden. They looked neither right nor left, nor did they hasten, but moved as one at an unearthly, dreamlike pace. Except that the performance was being given in the dark, there was nothing erratic or particularly covert in their actions. Just three men with parcels which cast spiky shadows on the grass. In moments they had reached the opposite border and glided into the trees. As before, the rectangle was empty of everything but moonlight and a breeze which gently rippled the surface of the pool.

I did sleep after all and woke the next morning to a brighter world. The air was clear, the sun was out, and the lawn looked green and innocent. Its only occupants were two elderly gardeners, tweaking and plucking their way through the shrubbery. By ten I was up on the hill with Michael and Ian Farr, who'd arrived with the crew.

Farr was thirtyish—tall, thin, and agitated in manner, but deliberate and droll in speech. "My colleague," he said, extending a hand to me. "I've looked forward to this meeting."

"Hello Ian," I said. "I hope I'm going to be helpful to you."

"I *know* you are," he answered, "and it won't be all nose-to-the-grindstone, darling. There are the cozier aspects of collaboration."

"I can hardly wait."

"Hey!" Michael interrupted.

"All right, old boy," Ian said. "No brusqueness, please. Come over here, sweet, and we'll run through the details of the finds. You know about the farm tools?" I nodded. "There's also a five-inch, ornamented bone plaque, found last month. I understand this has been exhilarating to the diggers, but we're going to have the devil's own time wringing drama from it on the tube. You've not seen it? We'll remedy that. Come along."

We began navigating the pitted surfaces of the plateau, Ian waving to members of the crew who were building camera platforms and trucking up the cumbersome paraphernalia of movie-making. I examined the bone plaque, the tools, the amphorae sherds and—plopped down on a breezy hillock—started smoothing out the script with Ian.

Our heads were still together when the sun shone straight overhead and a distant bell signaled lunch. All over the hillside people rose and stretched—some groaning—put tools aside and began making their way toward the tent. I had just gotten to my feet when Michael appeared with the announcement that we would have our meal in the village.

"Go ahead," said Ian, shuffling papers. "I'll catch up when I've organized these notes."

We started down. With Michael's hand on my elbow, I concentrated on not veering into tree limbs or falling into troughs while trying to decide if I should mention the garden prowlers. Twenty slippery steps later, I vetoed that idea. The details smacked of spinsterish imaginings. Who would believe another episode on the heels of the room search? In my mind's eye I saw these furtive figures on the lawn—slithering across with their odd packages. Attention to footwork slackened just then and I slipped in a rut, turning my ankle.

Michael's arms were fast around me in an instant—strong, his body warm but granite hard. Brown earth, sky, hands, shoulders—all jumbled as I was lifted high and carried to a pathside boulder. While Michael kneeled to probe ankle and foot, I stared at the top of his head—the dark hair inches away. I found I was yearning to be held again. At that moment touch was real, the Massachusetts hills a fantasy.

"You're lucky," Michael said, looking up. "No break."

"Oh. Good."

"But," he added, "I can see you're shaken. A hot bath is my prescription."

"Yes, doctor," I managed a smile. "And a little cup of tea?"

A look of real distress crossed his face. "The hill is steep, Beth. You might have been badly hurt."

"But I wasn't."

"Beth, don't you see? I brought you here . . . I feel responsible."

"You needn't."

"I don't understand your attitude. Surely you know that . . ."

He was going to say them—words that could change my life again. Sentences that would shackle me to emotions I thought I'd buried a long time ago. I wasn't ready. I might never be ready.

I cast about, groping for support, trying to stand. "Please, Michael, take me back."

He rose. "All right," was all he said as he hoisted me upright once more.

An hour later I lay in the mahogany bath, trying to squeeze real feeling from remembrance: his arm beneath my shoulders, my cheek against his chest. Pitiful, I thought. Pitiful to live on the fringes of—what?

12

The next few days were spent at the manor house. The ankle swelled and I limped a bit. It was Michael's edict that I not climb to the hilltop and I was not inclined to argue. Once seen, the dig did not have to be experienced daily and it was a relief to work at a table and chair. Ian gathered the on-site details and we put our heads together twice a day.

The house seemed strangely quiet. Sir Edmund and Benson had gone back to London in a limousine which, departing, looked like a giant beetle. With Sir Edmund away, Lily settled into an attitude short of convivial, but negotiable enough as social coin. Though Michael was busier than ever, the lines of tension had eased from his face. In rumpled corduroys and workshirt he strode in and out, marshalling the troops.

Peaceful enough, but all the same I felt bestirred and edgy. The work consumed a fraction of my day, my ankle inhibited outdoor walks, my sleep was troubled, my stomach upset. Most of this I attributed to my masquerade on Michael's behalf, but a portion of my nameless, formless fears I blamed on the house. Its size and coldness seemed to prevent a caring contact between its inhabitants—to set a better stage for nightly prowlers than for companionship. In this light, even Lily's cloying dependence on David was a relief of a kind. At least it offered some display of emotion, I decided, in this tight-lipped fastness of antiques.

This indulgent attitude prevailed until I was on my way to the study one afternoon, passing through the long corridor which ran behind the great hall. Books in hand, my mind fixed on the excavations, I came upon Lily wrapped in the arms of a lover. Under the heraldic glass and crewel hangings, they stood enmeshed—Lily murmuring words of endearment over and over and over again.

Then she saw me and pushed away—not from David, but from Michael. His face looked stern instead of ardent and it colored as he realized I was standing there. At that moment my eye caught a flicker of something in the gallery above and I saw David, like a vanishing phantom, bolt through a door. He had seen them too.

"Ah, Elizabeth," Michael said, "I was wondering where . . ."

"Hullo, Lily. Hullo, Michael," I countered in my best adolescent voice, and walked right by them. Lily's tinkling laughter followed until I firmly shut the study door.

I sat and found myself trembling. With what? Not anger, I felt too drained for that. Nor could I feel betrayed. I'd rejected my option on Michael's affections—someone else would fill that niche in his life. The realization stunned me—I'd once made peace with loneliness, now its misery was back. I knew David Cheney must be suffering as well. Stripped of his smooth urbanity, he'd looked as if someone had whipped him. Damn Lily, anyway.

For the next hour I simply moped, picked up the script and put it down again a dozen times, too rattled to work. Finally I decided that, ankle or no, I must have air. Air and at least some release from the claustrophobic tension. It would be tiresome to walk all the way upstairs, so I limped instead to the coat cupboard, which was itself the size of a small room, in search of something to wear outside. A dangling chain prompted a single light bulb above, and the light was poor. There was certainly an assortment of garments—sweaters, raincoats, duffle coats, a well-worn "British warm."

And a cloak. Of some heavy, rough, dark brown fiber. It hung toward the rear of the closet, and when I took it out I found it had a hood, no less. Intrigued, I slipped it on and examined myself in the door mirror. It was enormous, of course, hanging in folds at my feet, the pockets at knee level. I thrust my hands in these to pull the hem up from the floor, and my fingers closed on a knobby object on the right-hand side.

I drew it out and found a gold ring on my palm. In the dim cupboard light it appeared to be old, Tudor perhaps, and its bulbous top was scarred. I ran my fingers over it and thought it encrusted with something but—looking closer—discovered the uneven pattern was caused by some initials carved on the surface. Crudely carved, but then the ring was crude—hardly a prize acquisition. The initials were plain and deep, printed not scripted, without embellishment—N. A. They were initials which fit no one in the house. I felt the ring must have been misplaced by someone—the find of an afternoon's antique browse dropped and forgotten. I tucked it into my sweater pocket, planning to show it around when the group had gathered, and pulled on an old duffle coat for my walk.

The gardens were rain soaked and soggy, the gravel path squished underfoot. I made the circuit once with my ankle aching, then sat in the mist on a wooden bench. At home when I felt blue there were low-key remedies: a chat with a student, an outing to Boston. Here I felt estranged and isolated, deprived of touchstones. While I sat steeped in misery it began to rain again, and finally the exercise seemed more a punishment than an airing. I hobbled back to the house.

Michael was waiting in the hall. "I was just about to bring you an umbrella."

"I find the rain refreshing."

"But you're soaked. Here," he began unbuttong the coat, "let's get this off."

"Michael, I'm an adult. I can undress myself."

He stopped. "You don't sound like an adult now. You sound about twelve."

"*I* sound twelve!"

"Elizabeth, I know what you're thinking, but you're wrong. The episode in the hall—it wasn't what it seemed to be."

"Michael, what you choose to do is really none of my business." Priggish. The words sounded priggish, but it was too late to bite them back.

"Now, just a minute." He pulled off the coat and flung it to the floor. "You're going to listen to me, Beth. This is important to us both." He held me at arm's length. "First Lily. She surprised me."

I simply stared.

"I mean it, Beth. We met in the hall and we'd been talking just a minute when she threw her arms around my neck."

"I see."

"I'm telling you the truth. What could I do, push her away? She's been so unstable lately that she might not be able to handle that kind of rejection."

"I'm going up now." I retrieved the coat and turned toward the hall. Michael walked beside me.

At the cupboard door he pulled the light chain, casting shadows all about us, and I groped past sodden garments to find an empty hook. The clothing seemed a woolen forest, with undergrowth of boots and fishing gear. I found a peg far in the back.

"Beth," Michael said, "you can't believe Lily means anything to me."

He was blocking the door. "Michael, please."

"In Wales I'd sit up through the night thinking of our time together. I remembered how you loved me . . . and how little that meant to me then."

"That was years ago."

"I had to meet a lot of shoddy people before I realized how true you were. You never questioned what we had. I never had to pretend with you . . . or try to be something that terrified me. I came back to New York and tried to find you, but you'd evaporated."

I stood silent, remembering the flowers that had filled my apartment. I'd never touched them. They'd faded to stalks in their vases when I left to begin life again.

"I called your parents once. I knew they'd never mention that to you. They were distant, protective. I don't blame them, but I felt as though a door had been slammed in my face. The day I found you in the street I couldn't believe my luck. I hoped the opportunity to work together . . . to *be* together . . . would help us both. I hoped we'd have another chance."

"Chance?" I said levelly. "A chance for what?"

I thought he'd wince, but he smiled instead, a smile so filled with regret and tenderness that my heart turned over.

"Let's give it time," he said. "Meanwhile, if I don't deserve your love, maybe I can earn affection. Will you be my friend, Beth?"

"Yes, Michael. Yes." I felt so tired. "I'll be your friend."

Back in my room, I paced at first—ignoring the pile of books Ian had provided. But finally I sat down and managed to complete a decent amount of work before dinner. The filming had begun, and we felt pressed to stay ahead of the cameras. Actually the rest of the script was simple—a summing-up of the aims of the dig, the aspirations of the diggers, and the hopes for other excavations throughout Britain.

Michael had originally thought Sir Edmund might do a portion of the sum-up, but this was now out of the question. Gamble, we decided, wasn't "right." He could serve as a family representative as well as overseer, but his credentials were thin and his glibness might strike the wrong note. Finally, Ian decided to have an actor come down from London to do the end narration. Having him stand on Thorn Hill and recite seemed a cliché, but I did not know how to get around that. Anyway, script style was Ian's province; I was there to check the facts.

"Plump up the meat of it, darling." Ian had said, "I'll add the curlicues." Then he'd added, "I hope you're staying until the bitter end . . . until what's-his-name from London drops the final word."

"I don't know, Ian. I thought I'd leave as soon as my work is done."

"It would only be two or three days longer. Do stay, Elizabeth—for your own satisfaction. It's unusual to be able to follow a job throughout. It's good for the emotions—puts a period on the work in a most gratifying way." I hadn't responded, but privately felt that I would keep to my plan: finish and slip away at the first opportunity.

It was about seven when I looked up from my books. Too late to bathe and change. I combed my hair quickly and dabbed on some lipstick so I wouldn't look the total frump, then joined the familiar cast in the dining room. They were playing their parts in true form: Gamble sardonic, Lily arch and brittle, David civilized but distant. Only Ian lent a lighter touch, and I heard Michael laughing with him at the end of the table. There were empty chairs down there but I sat near the head, next to Tom Marsden.

He looked less dour somehow, then I realized there was no blue jaw; he must have shaved that afternoon. He turned towards me, unsmiling as always.

"How is the ankle tonight?"

"Much better, thanks. I seem to be limping less."

"Tricky climb, that, up to the dig."

"You've been up? I thought you were more or less bound to the manor."

He shifted in his chair and slowly scanned the room before he answered. "I've been up once. Just to see."

"Are you from these parts, Mr. Marsden?"

"I'm from Yorkshire."

"Ah. The moors?"

"No. Ramsgill-in-Nidderdale."

"Sounds picturesque."

"It's a tiny place. All farmland—very quiet."

"That's where you worked before coming here?"

"I ran a big place outside Ripon. The lads in the family took off for other parts, so I managed it for two women." The way he said "women" made them sound like a pair of wing-sheared birds, flapping on the turf. I could see it was going to be one of those uphill conversations. I flaked my lemon sole and had another try.

"I find Thorn Hill House and the village very beautiful. They seem . . ."

He interrupted. "Yes, it's nice here," and turned to his fish. That was that. There was no more talk as we progressed through salad, pudding, coffee. At that point, even the subdued clatter of fork on plate, cup against saucer, were beginning to get on my nerves. I was sniffling, too. The turn in the garden had practically insured a cold. I reached into my sweater pocket for a handkerchief and felt instead the knobby ring. I pulled it out.

"Mr. Marsden?"

He looked at me with thinly veiled impatience. "Yes?"

"I found something this afternoon which I think may belong to someone here." I held the ring out on my palm. "Does it look familiar? Do you think . . . ?"

What happened next was so unexpected that my words were

chopped midway. Marsden's hand shot out and gripped my outstretched one, closing it, crushing the fingers tight around the ring. The pain was so extreme that I gasped, then clenched my teeth to keep from crying out. Slowly, steadily, his eyes searching mine, that stare ordering compliance, Marsden pulled me toward him and when our heads were close he whispered furiously, "Put that bloody thing away. Do you hear me? Keep it hidden."

There was an odd metallic taste in my mouth from clamped jaw and grinding teeth. I must have paled. Marsden dropped my hand as abruptly as he had snatched it up, but in no way seemed remorseful.

"Put it away," he repeated.

I did as I was told, ever so slowly letting my hand drop to lap and pocket, painfully unfolding my bent fingers, sliding the ring out of sight. I needed a moment to compose myself and, when I seemed to be breathing normally again, ventured a look around the table. Most of the diners were chattering away, but down at the end Michael was leaning forward, looking toward me, both elbows on the table as if he were about to rise and walk over.

To forestall this, I quickly rose myself, murmured something, turned, and left. All I wanted at that moment was to get safely back to my room. I walked through the darkened hall, passing the serving trolleys, hearing bits of conversation from the kitchen, feeling—in drafts—the autumn chill which had crept in from the countryside. I was halfway to the staircase when I heard an urgent tapping of footsteps-on-stone behind me. That would be Michael, and I did not want to see him. I quickened my pace and the footsteps hastened too. I was at the bottom of the staircase, just about to go up, when someone touched my shoulder.

"Oh!"

"Don't be startled," said Tom Marsden. "It's just me. I wanted to apologize. I hope I didn't hurt your hand."

I wanted to say, Damn you . . . you hurt it quite a lot, but the need to run took precedence, so I answered, "That's all right. Good night."

"Wait."

I turned again.

"The ring is mine," Marsden said, "a family heirloom. I'm fond of it, which is why I keep it with me and not in a vault somewhere . . . it's a kind of lucky piece. I'd . . . misplaced it . . . and it startled me when you brought it out." He looked at me intently. "Frankly, I'd rather it wasn't seen by anyone. I'm concerned someone might think it a find on the property. One I'd just appropriated."

His explanation was so transparently false that I simply stared back at him for a moment. Then I fished in my pocket and pulled out the ring. "Here. Take it please."

"Thanks. I'll keep it safe this time and . . . by the way . . . I'd appreciate your not mentioning this to anyone."

"Mr. Marsden," it took some discipline to keep an even tone, "my only interest in the ring was to return it to its owner. Since you say you are that person, I feel my responsibility is discharged."

He faded back into the corridor as I climbed the stairs, indignation mounting with the steps. I'd been given, I decided, another sterling reason for flight.

13

Sidney Bullock was not well equipped for subterfuge. Tall, thickly built, and pallid, he was accustomed to thumping through life—the pale face swaying above other heads, the body sidling like a cantankerous machine. He was aware that his appearance made him vulnerable to mockery, and saw the man sitting opposite was studying him now. That made him uncomfortable.

The man had introduced himself as Baker, then had sat back, staring. Periodically he ran his tongue along his lip, as if soothing a canker there. Bullock didn't like him and he didn't like the room they shared: a dump of an office high in a warehouse block. The elevator had been an open platform which shuddered as it rose.

He heard the platform descend again and half turned to listen, but Baker gave no sign. Presently there were voices, hollow and echoing in the loft. Three men came in.

"Sidney," Littell said.

"Good evening, Edmund."

Benson propped an attaché case against a drafting board and took Sir Edmund's coat. The third man folded his and put it on a chair. He looked European—Polish or German. Two strangers, Bullock thought.

Benson spread a map of London across the drawing board and Littell leaned his outstretched hand upon it.

"Will you step up, Sidney, and point out the locations? Mr. . . ."

"Baker."

"Mr. Baker will have a look too."

Bullock took off his hat and lumbered to the table. With a pencil-end as pointer, he described the sites in an elliptical sweep, ending at a point south of London. "And Brixton," he concluded.

"Brixton, the major site," Sir Edmund said to Baker. "How many men there, Sidney?"

"Two hundred of ours at the crucial spots, a thousand sympathizers."

Baker frowned. "We'll need double the number of weapons then."

Bullock seemed stunned. "Weapons?"

"This isn't a Hyde Park romp," Baker snapped. "Yes, weapons. Rifles, guns, grenades."

"You'll have them," Littell said. "What about your people?"

"Newcastle, Liverpool, and Birmingham. All arranged."

"Excellent."

Bullock put on his hat. "I have to leave."

"All right, Sidney," Littell turned to Baker. "I suggest you go along with Mr. Bullock and work out his requirements . . ."

"I thought . . ."

"Not now," Benson said.

Baker shrugged and walked out. Bullock was already on his way to the elevator, as if trying to put maximum distance between them.

Littell stared after Bullock and said to no one in particular, "He had a fine record in the war."

"Sir?"

"He was brave. Knew no fear at all. His constituents remember that."

The European coughed, and Littell added casually, "On this other matter . . . you're experienced?"

"Yes, sir."

"Where are you staying?"

"At a hotel near the Embankment."

"You know the Secretary's schedule?"

"Yes, sir."

Benson began folding up the map.

"Will it be quick?"

"He'll never know."

"That's merciful."

14

I rose very early the next morning, hoping to work while my mind was clear. I was now counting script pages as dates on a calendar whizzing toward some superlunary deliverance day. Sally must have heard my typewriter. She delivered a breakfast tray at seven, but was back again before I'd had two bites of toast.

"It's the phone, miss."

"For me? At this hour?

"It's Dr. Trehane, miss. He says it's urgent that he speak to you."

I ran downstairs to the telephone alcove. Geoffrey's voice was tense, and he got quickly to the point.

"Elizabeth. I need to see you right away."

"Now?"

"Shortly. I've found something you should know about. Is Michael there?"

"I haven't seen him. He must have left, though, Geoffrey. They start filming early."

"Bring him along if you can find him without arousing curiosity. If not, come yourself."

"Where . . . and when?"

"Meet me at the stationer's at ten. It's also the post office and I normally go by there at that time."

"I'll be there."

"And Elizabeth."

"Yes?"

"If you're telling this to Michael, make sure no one else is listening. When will Edmund be back?"

"On Saturday, I believe."

"I see. Well . . . until ten then. Elizabeth?" There was the slightest quaver in his voice.

"Yes, Geoffrey?"

"You won't fail me, will you?"

I gave him all the assurance I could and put down the phone confounded. What could he have found and why should it mandate all this secrecy? Geoffrey had been tired lately, worn thin by his projects and what he considered to be his responsibilities to Sir Edmund. But he was not fatigued enough to breed delusions—that hearty exterior was matched, I was sure, by an iron constitution and a healthy mind. Assuming the problem was genuine, what could Thorn Hill hold that would cause such anxiety?

By nine-thirty I was peddling toward the village on Sally's bicycle. Michael had left early, as I thought, and I did not want to generate curiosity by requesting a car. At the stationer's there was a cozy intermingling of tobacco, newsprint, and toffee smells—but no Geoffrey. The proprietress and I exchanged empty smiles while I examined paperbacks and remarked—twice—about the weather. By ten-forty, the smiles had attenuated into grimace and the purchased paperbacks had grown to five. Geoffrey's cautions echoed in my head and I was wary of asking after him directly, but as the time lengthened, my worries grew. What could be keeping him?

Just after eleven, I finally gave in. "Pardon me, Mrs. . . ."

"Gray," she responded. "I'm Helen Gray."

"Elizabeth Kendall. I'm working with a film company here and staying at the manor."

"Yes, I know." She smiled again. "You were pointed out to me."

Pointed out.

"I see. Well!" I tried to sound lighthearted. "Dr. Trehane arranged to meet me here this morning—we were going to do some sightseeing—and now I'm wondering what's become of him."

"Odd, isn't it?" she said. "I'm standing here wondering the same thing. Dr. Trehane comes by each morning no later than ten past ten. He's what my husband calls a 'clockwork person'—someone you can set your watch by."

"Punctual."

"Absolutely. Look, my dear," she pointed toward the rear of the shop. "There's a telephone back there, why don't you ring him? Wait." She scribbled on a piece of paper. "Here's the number. Call him now."

I walked back to the phone and dialed the number. After the usual grinds and whirrings, the signal began. It rang and rang, but no one picked up.

"Mrs. Gray," I called out.

"Yes?"

"No answer."

"Now that's *really* odd," she said, obviously concerned. "Even if Dr. Trehane is out, Mrs. Tierney should be there. She does the house every morning but Sunday. You're sure you rang correctly?"

"I believe so. Would you try, Mrs. Gray."

"I will," she said, and repeated the exercise with the same results. "No answer," she confirmed, then added, "Oh my dear, I'm sorry. I've kept you standing all this time." She pulled a stool from behind the counter. "I heard you'd hurt your leg on the hill, and you've been on your feet here for an hour."

"It was my ankle, and it's better now. Thank you, Mrs. Gray, but I won't wait. If the professor comes, will you tell him I've been here and have gone back to the manor?"

"Of course I will," she patted my hand. "Don't worry, Miss Kendall, he'll turn up. I'm sure there's some . . ."

"Reasonable explanation?"

"Yes. Reasonable explanation. That's what they always say, isn't it?"

"Yes. That's what they say."

I spent a brooding, uneasy day at the manor house, alternately peering out the window and running downstairs to try Geoffrey at the number Mrs. Gray had given me. Through the afternoon I was tempted to go to his house and look myself, but finally decided against that approach. The village of Thorn Hill was like other hamlets everywhere. I'd been "pointed out" to Mrs. Gray; she knew I was staying at the manor and had "hurt my leg" on the hill. Presumably she and her neighbors also knew what brand of toothpaste I favored and who cut my hair. Going to Geoffrey's house would mean I'd have to pedal through the village, advertising my anxiety and attracting attention, which was precisely what Geoffrey had asked me to avoid.

The weather seemed to mirror my apprehension, turning bleak. The fields and gardens, which seemed so charming in the sunshine, looked stark and chilled. I put on an old cardigan, buttoned it once at the neck, and pulled it around me—the sleeves dangling—fashioning a small cocoon of warmth and solace. About three it began to drizzle and fifteen minutes later, Michael's car came up the drive. I flew downstairs to meet him.

"Raining," he said, "so we closed up early. Rotten day, anyhow. Too overcast . . ."

"Michael, I must speak to you."

He was alert at once. "Beth, you're all wound up. What's the trouble?"

I told him. "There's still no answer," I concluded, "and not another word from him all day."

Michael was frowning. "That's strange. He specifically said he had *found* something, not noticed . . . or observed?"

"Found was the word he used. And he wanted me to be quiet about meeting him. He said to bring you only if I could do so without attracting attention."

"I see. Anything else?"

"He did ask when Sir Edmund would be back. When I told him he didn't seem surprised. It was as though he knew it would be Saturday and just wanted confirmation."

"Well," Michael stood up. "The first thing we're going to do—right now—is drive over there. The phone may be out of order."

"I checked with the exchange. It's not."

"We'll go anyway. Get your coat."

We were hurrying through the hall when the doorbell chimed and the butler stepped in front of us to admit a doughty little person in a black raincoat and black hat—Mrs. Tierney. Her voice was low, but tremulous, and we could see her struggling to keep calm. I took her ice-cold hands in mine and drew her to a fire.

She seemed better when she'd warmed a bit. "The Constable and I have looked everywhere, you see," she said, "and he simply cannot be found. I thought someone here at the manor might help me. I . . . ," she paused and swallowed, "I didn't know where else to go."

"You were quite right to come here, Mrs. Tierney," Michael said. He laid a consoling hand on her shoulder and asked, "Would you please tell us . . . step by step . . . everything that's happened since this morning?"

"Since this morning," she parroted nervously. "Yes, I will. I came to work as usual this morning at half-past nine. I make Dr. Trehane's breakfast before I do anything else. He just has tea when he gets up, then I make him a regular breakfast—bacon and eggs, you know. He doesn't take much for lunch—just cheese and fruit—so he stokes up in the morning. Well, this morning he wasn't downstairs when I got there, so I thought he was upstairs working."

"Or had slept late?" Michael interjected.

Mrs. Tierney looked faintly indignant. "He *never* slept late, sir. He was an early riser. He was always up and . . . ," she blushed, "*dressed* when I arrived."

"Of course, Mrs. Tierney," I said soothingly, "we understand." I shot a chiding look to Michael.

"Anyway," she continued, "I made the breakfast as usual and when it was ready I realized there was no sound upstairs . . . no walking around . . . so I went to the staircase and called up. There was no answer. I got worried then, thinking he might have fallen or gone sick in the night. So I went up and . . . ," she looked from me to Michael, "he wasn't there."

"He called me about seven, Mrs. Tierney," I told her. "So he must have been in the house at that time . . . unless he phoned from somewhere else."

"Why would he do that?" she asked, puzzled.

"I can't think of any reason. There's just that possibility."

"What did you do then . . . when you realized he wasn't there?" Michael asked.

"I went out into the garden, thinking he might be pruning the hedge or some such thing, but the garden was empty. So I started my housework, imagining he would come home." Mrs. Tierney turned toward me, her eyes filled with distress. "But he didn't come. It was all so . . . so unlike him, miss. Four years last May it's been since I began keeping Dr. Trehane's house and he *never* changed the routine without telling me in advance. If he planned a trip, he'd tell me days before. If he just stepped out on an errand, he'd leave a message on the kitchen table."

"So you called the Constable," Michael said.

"I asked the neighbors first and then walked through the village myself. I've been out most of the day . . . just looking. When it got past noon and I'd been everywhere, I went to the Constable. He and the two men from the garage looked around the base of the hill and in the fields behind the house, but . . . they had no luck."

I glanced at my watch. It was almost four. If there was to be another search, it would have to be done right away, in the hour or so of daylight left.

Michael seemed to have read my mind. "We'll have another look," he said briskly. "We'll put more men on the job. The crew will help, I know, and maybe the students will too."

Mrs. Tierney sagged back in sheer relief. "If you *would* do that, sir. I'm so worried that he may be hurt."

I leaned down and gave her what I hoped was an encouraging hug. "We'll do all we can. Why don't you stay here? It will be better for you than waiting alone."

We got Geoffrey's house key from Mrs. Tierney and settled her in a wing chair with some words of comfort. The moment we were out of earshot, Michael said, "We'll have to move fast. If he *is* hurt and not found before nightfall, I wouldn't give much for his chances."

"Oh, Michael."

"Well, what's your diagnosis?" He looked at me and added tersely, "Does he seem the kind of man who would take off without leaving a word?"

"Of course not."

"There you are. He's in trouble, and it's *very* late," Michael said. His pace quickened. "I'll round up the crew and speak to Gamble. He should be able to contribute a dozen men. You call the Constable . . . we'll want him to work with us."

Long afterwards, when I thought of that afternoon, what I remembered was a line of men moving through the fields behind the village. Spaced a few feet apart and armed with sticks, branches, broom handles—anything that could probe into bramble and thicket—they moved over open ground and through woodland, checking verges and ditches, poking into hawthorn hedges and decaying stumps, scattering papery sycamore seeds, flushing a skunk of foxes who bounded—agitated—into the brush. Michael, Keith Gamble, and a very young, slowly unraveling Constable Mickle directed the moves. One squad was dispatched to a nearby quarry and came back on the double, relieved to have found it empty.

My sense of dread grew as night approached. With light failing and no results, the pace of the search increased. The men walked quickly and they no longer poked with their sticks. They flailed instead, swinging them backwards and forwards over the ground, thrashing at bushes and trees. Dusk passed into evening. There was a futile attempt to continue the search using lanterns, but the radius of the lantern light was inadequate to the job. Slowly, first one by one and then in teams, the men dispersed, leaving the Constable, Michael, Keith Gamble, and me—a soggy little group—standing in a pitch-black field. A few moments later Michael and I got into the car for a wordless drive back to the manor. The search was over.

15

We arrived to find that Mrs. Tierney had been taken home—a blessing for me. All the way down the darkened roads and up the drive I had worried about facing her. What could I say that would temper her anxiety now? How could she rest in her own snug house knowing Geoffrey might be lying outside somewhere—crumpled, helpless, possibly dying? How could any of us rest?

Michael was saying little, but I knew we shared the same forebodings. Geoffrey had called to say he'd found something, then had disappeared. There had to be a connection between those facts and I racked my brain to reconstruct every phrase of our conversation. Was there something he'd said—softly, obliquely—which I'd overlooked?

The next hours were pained and fidgety. The phone rang twice and Michael answered: Constable Mickle was reporting—disappointingly—on dead-end leads. Mostly we sat across the study from each other chewing separate kernels of surmise, smiling blankly and reflexively from time to time, our coats dumped on a nearby chair so we could pick up and run if summoned. I saw

Michael nodding once or twice, his head dipping toward his folded arms; each time he caught himself, stretched, and yawned. It was after ten when he murmured something about calling it a day.

"I don't think I could sleep, Michael."

"Aren't you tired?"

"Of course . . . but can't we wait a bit longer?"

"Beth," he said quietly, "we're not going to hear anything else tonight."

"I know. I know. I suppose you're right. There's not much point in sitting here, but . . . "

"All right. We'll wait a little longer."

I turned to watch the fire prance behind the grate, mindful of its warmth, the comfort of my chair, my dry boots, Michael's presence. Geoffrey would be alone now—all alone in pitiable conditions. The scrape of tree branch on windowpane reminded me of the night outside—the bone-chilling damp and the wind. Scrape, scrape. No light, no comfort, no other living thing to help with fright or pain. Scrape, scrape.

The angels. The stone angels in the church had taken off their halos and were using them as tambourines. Bang. Bang. They were standing upright in the chancel, tapping on the tambourines, tapping out a welcome. A welcome to *where?* A welcome to *whom?* Why they were welcoming Geoffrey, of course, welcoming him to heaven. The little church rang with the sound and the tambourines flashed. Bang. Bang. The church . . .

"Michael!" I was out of the chair and pulling at him before I was fully awake. "Michael!"

"Beth." He was on his feet. "Beth, you've been sleeping, dreaming . . . "

"The church, Michael. Have you looked in the church?"

"The church?" he echoed blankly.

"Not the big one . . . the little one down the back lane. Did you . . . did anyone look there?"

"I looked myself with two boys. Not inside, it was locked, but we went all around it and up and down that lane . . . through every hedge, in every ditch . . . "

"But not inside?"

"No. But surely if Geoffrey were sitting in there he would have heard us. We made enough noise."

"Michael, I just have a feeling. We must look in that church."

"How do you plan to do that? It's locked."

"Geoffrey had a key."

"If he had a key and used it for admittance, it's in there with him."

"Perhaps, but maybe it's still at his place. The cottage is on the way. We could stop there and look for it. Oh Michael, couldn't we try? Anything is better than just sitting here."

"I agree," Michael held my coat and I slipped into it, "but promise me when we get back you'll go to bed."

"I will. I promise."

We got back in the car and sped through the village again—a village now shuttered and locked for the day, with only the pub lights piercing the darkness. I had seen Geoffrey's home in the daytime—a plain, off-white stone cottage with thatch replaced by glazed pantiles. It held more utility than charm, but Geoffrey was proud of its modern conveniences. I was reminded of that when I flipped the electric switch inside the door and the light went on to reveal a cottage interior with a literary tinge. Books were piled everywhere and a rather decrepit old desk stood on the brick floor in one corner, its top filled with papers in teetering piles. Beyond that, there was the usual polished brass, checkered curtains, and tidy hearth, all no doubt tended admirably by Mrs. Tierney.

Michael was rummaging at some pegs near the door. "Isn't this what he was wearing when we saw him last?"

It was Geoffrey's old jacket, sagging and mended. As Michael held it out I thought how much it *looked* like Geoffrey, how it had taken on his shape and personality.

"That's it."

"I've looked through the other stuff . . . this is the last," Michael said, delving into the pockets. "Nothing."

"I guess finding the key was too much to hope for."

"I'm afraid so, Beth, but we'll still have a look at the church. There must . . . hey!" Replacing the jacket, Michael had paused. He pulled something off one of the wooden pegs and turned to show it to me. It was a group of keys, held by a loop of discolored string. One of the keys, rusted and elderly, was larger than the rest.

"The church key?" Michael asked.

"Yes! At least it could be."

"Let's go."

The lane leading to the church seemed more circuitous at night. Michael's car grazed the hedgerows twice and he cursed each time. I sat rigid in my seat, peering out at the stretch lit by the car lights, hypnotized by the speed we were traveling and half sick with tension. The darkness was so complete that the church appeared as a black blur, a hunched stone pile. Michael brought a torch from the car and we walked to the door. The key fitted.

The hush inside was absolute. We crossed the church porch into the nave, moving cautiously on the rough-paved flooring. Michael flashed his light over the silent row of wooden chairs. I shivered.

"Are you all right?" he asked.

"It's clammy in here."

We walked on, Michael slightly in front of me, rotating the torch. We had just moved into the chancel when he stopped.

"What is it?"

"There's something ahead," he answered. "Stay put."

"Something? Where?"

"On the floor. Stay here, Beth."

I froze. Michael moved again, his back blocking the torch-light, then he stopped again.

"What is it, Michael? What's there?"

A whisper came back—a whisper I hardly recognized as Michael's voice.

"It's Geoffrey."

"Geoffrey?" I stepped forward.

"*Don't* Beth. I don't think you should see . . . "

But I had already seen what was sprawled on the floor in the fierce yellow beam of the torch. There on his side, with one arm stretched out—the hand curled like a supplicant's—lay Geoffrey Trehane. His jaw was slack and his eyes were open, staring upward. They were empty—fixed in the catatonia of death.

16

The following hours were a jumbled nightmare. Michael hustled me out of the church at once and sent me off in the car for Constable Mickle, while he stood guard at the door. I cried all the way—partly in horror and partly in anguished pity for Geoffrey, whom we had left in the dark again.

Sometime that night I got to bed, but slept only fitfully—I could not get warm and I could not stop shaking. In the morning I came downstairs to find knots of people standing about in the hall. Maids were distributing cups of coffee and bits of breakfast, but the atmosphere was so doleful that no one appeared to be eating.

I was surprised to see Benson, who hurried over—perspiring as usual—to relay the news. He had arrived from London with Sir Edmund about two in the morning, he said, and the police squad had appeared shortly afterwards. Michael had just gone to bed. He'd been with the police all night, going over the scene in the church. When daylight came he had gone to Mrs. Tierney's home to break the news himself.

"The Superintendent decided not to disturb your rest," Benson added, "but he is anxious to speak with you this morning."

"The Superintendent?"

"Detective Chief Superintendent Whitelaw. He is heading the investigative team."

Whitelaw was waiting for me—a powerfully framed, impassive man in a smooth brown suit. His eyes were two gray stones. He seated me and began his questions in a solemn tone.

"I realize all this must have been shocking to you, Miss Kendall," he said. "It's shocking to *us.* It's rare that a crime of this type occurs in a village like Thorn Hill."

Then it had been no accident.

"I'm sorry, Superintendent. I just saw Geoffrey . . . Dr. Trehane . . . for a moment in the church. I . . . we . . . could tell he was dead, but I didn't know he had been . . ."

"You didn't know he had been murdered," Whitelaw said flatly. "In point of fact, Dr. Trehane was killed by a heavy blow to the back of the head which caused linear fractures and hemorrhage. This was performed by the classic blunt instrument . . . a weapon which we have not yet found. In street parlance someone crept up . . . or more likely ran lightly up behind him . . . and bashed him."

Something churned at the pit of my stomach.

"Since you were apparently the last person to speak to Dr. Trehane," Whitelaw continued, "we now need your fullest cooperation."

"Of course. I'll do anything I can."

"Good. Perhaps you'll begin by telling me the gist of your telephone conversation."

I went over it phrase by phrase and then—at Whitelaw's direction—virtually word by word. When I had finished he sat quite still at the desk. Only the fingers of one hand moved over its polished top as though they might knead structure and reason into my answers.

"I know it's not much," I said.

"It doesn't *appear* to be much," he responded. "We'll see. You're sure he said he had found something?"

"Oh, yes. He said he'd found something I should know about. I remember quite clearly. Michael and I discussed that while Geoffrey was missing."

"I wonder, Miss Kendall, why it was something *you* should know about? Not Mr. Grandville or Sir Edmund . . . nor anyone else . . . but you specifically."

"I don't know, except . . ."

"Except what?"

"We *did* share an interest in various historical periods. I can't see a discovery in that field would call for secrecy, though."

"Nor can I. The keys are another puzzling item. Since they were found in the cottage, how did Dr. Trehane get into the church? No keys were found on the body. Did he have more than one church key?"

"I don't know," I said doubtfully. "I don't think so. Geoffrey showed me the church when I arrived in Thorn Hill. At the time he mentioned that few people had access to it. He implied that just he and Sir Edmund had keys."

"I see. Dr. Trehane also asked when Sir Edmund would be returning from London. Do you think . . . did you get the impression . . . that he intended to share his 'find' with him?"

"No."

"No?"

"That is, I believe he was asking about Sir Edmund to verify when he would be returning. I really couldn't say whether he intended to share any information with him. It's so hard to judge that sort of thing from tone of voice."

"Indeed it is, Miss Kendall. Let's leave that kind of speculation for a while then, and concentrate on what we know. What made you think of looking in the church, for instance? Mr. Grandville said you fairly bolted from your chair."

"I was dreaming."

"He explained that. But your feeling about the church must have been very strong . . . to prod you awake like that."

What *had* propelled me out of the dream?

"I'm not sure, but I think it was Geoffrey's strong affection for the church which made me dream of it last night. The afternoon he guided me through it . . . the way he felt about it . . . had made a deep impression."

"It was not unnatural for him to be there then . . . alone?"

"No. He generally went alone. But the time . . . I would think it would be unnatural for him to be there at that time of night."

"Dr. Trehane had been dead for hours when you found him," Whitelaw said. "Our police surgeon believes he died about the time he planned to meet you."

I had a sudden image of Geoffrey being probed and photographed—and carted away in a rubber sheet. A hum began in my ears, faint at first, then gradually louder. I leaned forward and put my head in my hands.

"Miss Kendall."

I heard the Superintendent's voice, sensed he was standing beside me—and then felt two strong hands. One held my shoulder and the other gripped the back of my neck and forced my head down past my knees. I seemed to hang there forever, while the hum came and went. Finally the room cleared and Whitelaw pulled me upright again. His face was grave.

"I'm sorry all this is so upsetting to you. Perhaps . . . in light of the shock you've had . . . we should postpone this interview until later today."

"No. Please." The thought of starting over was unbearable. "I'm fine now. Let's go on."

"Well then," he sat at the desk again. "I'll try to be brief. Do you think there's a chance someone overheard your conversation with Dr. Trehane?"

"Overheard? I don't see how. The telephone alcove is fairly private."

"Yes, I've seen it. It seems the paneling would soundproof it effectively. I understand it was Sir Edmund's father's wish that telephones do not jangle all over the house. I believe the only other telephones are in Sir Edmund's quarters."

"If you are thinking of extensions, I don't think there was any interference on the line."

"And there was no one nearby at the time of the call?"

"I saw no one."

"I see. Miss Kendall, would you explain your position in this film venture. Your function, that is."

Function, indeed. I suppose I knew that sooner or later—in one form or another—that question would be put to me.

"I am a technical adviser."

"That entails script supervision?"

"I work with the writer, yes."

"You are qualified to do this work? You've done it before?"

He's already covered this ground with Michael, I thought. It's our relationship he's really probing.

"I am a teacher on sabbatical to do some research here in England, Superintendent. The period covered in the documentary is a period of history I teach at home. Michael . . . Mr. Grandville . . . asked me to help with the script here."

"You did not come to England for that purpose then?"

"No. Michael and I ran into each other in London." I paused. "We are old friends."

"And this work has kept you more or less occupied since you arrived at Thorn Hill?"

"Yes. I've been busy with Ian Farr."

Whitelaw rose again—in the even, graceful way some large men have—and walked to the window. He stood for a moment, looking out, then turned to me.

"You can understand our feelings of puzzlement, Miss Kendall. We must question every one this way. Quiet, well-respected men like Dr. Trehane do not die violent deaths—they die peacefully in bed. And the setting of the murder is queer indeed.

"An empty Saxon church is an unlikely place for a burglary. There's nothing to prize from those walls. There's no reason for the odd criminal to go there and it would be bizarre for a man seeking spiritual comfort to get up off his knees to bludgeon Dr. Trehane. Mrs. Tierney says he carried next to nothing in his pockets."

That was characteristic. Geoffrey, who thought treasures abounded in books and in the tranquil countryside, would have no need for cash in wads—or a plastic clutch of credit cards.

Whitelaw shuffled a few papers on the desk. "I guess that covers the preliminaries, Miss Kendall. You will keep yourself available today, though? Stay close to the house in case I need you?"

"I will."

And that was that. I left the study mindful of the word "preliminaries." That meant a string of interviews would follow—something I didn't want to think about. I went out curiously relieved, however. In a sense the talk had been unburdening—all my troubled thoughts and strained conjectures had been lodged with the Superintendent.

Michael appeared shortly after two. He smelled of soap and after-shave, but his face was crumpled and his eyes tired.

"I can never sleep in the daytime," he explained.

"And today . . . ," I began.

"Right. Not one of your better days in any case."

I ran through the morning with him, and my interview with Whitelaw.

He listened, then said solemnly, "Beth, I'm doing my best to get you out of here."

"Out of here?"

"Back to London. As quickly as possible. We only have two days of shooting left anyway. Your work is done."

"I don't know, Michael," I said doubtfully. "Superintendent Whitelaw asked me to keep myself available. He said available *today,* but I think that could easily be extended to the rest of the week. There are so many details to clear up . . . or to put in focus."

"Whitelaw's a tough bird," Michael conceded, "but I think I can get him to let you leave."

"Michael," I said slowly. "I don't know whether I want to do that."

"Why not?"

"Perhaps I feel I have an obligation."

"An obligation to *whom,* for God's sake?"

"An obligation to Geoffrey." Saying it made me feel better—made me feel contained and purposeful. "I know he's dead. I know nothing touches him now. But his spirit . . . someone must pay homage to his spirit. It would seem uncaring to just leave."

Michael's voice was husky. "Beth . . ."

"And the cottage," I continued. "There will be things at the cottage which need tending. I could help with that."

"All right, sweetheart." Michael touched a forefinger to my shoulder and ran it down along my arm. "You do what you think best, but you will be very careful, won't you?"

"Yes, Michael. Of course I will."

Careful—full of care. As I went upstairs I wondered how one could walk charily at Thorn Hill, where one was disarmed at every turn by the solid weight of centuries. The manor and the village had stood through a thousand seasons and more: summers, winters, falls, and springs—each with their particular delights unfolding. As the Superintendent said, it was inconceivable that murder should happen here and evil flourish.

Absorbed, I almost missed my bedroom door, then caught

myself, walked in—and stopped. Sally was standing in the middle of the room. She held a package in her hand.

"Sally!"

She flushed. "I hope I didn't startle you, miss."

"Not really." She seemed unnaturally poised, as if the package were something she wanted to heave into a corner. "I was just surprised to see you."

"It's this parcel, miss." She appeared to be genuinely embarrassed. "I . . . I was just about to leave it for you."

"Yes?"

"But I didn't want to *just* leave it . . . that is, leave it without an explanation. I was looking about for a paper and pencil so I could leave a note with it."

"Why a note? Is there a problem?"

"It was left in your cubby for you, miss. The only problem . . . the reason for the note . . . is to tell you that the parcel must have been sitting for a day. I didn't look in your cubby yesterday. I'm sorry, Miss Kendall," she added anxiously. "Yesterday was so busy. Cook asked me to help make sandwiches for the search party and with one thing or another, I was running the whole time."

"Is that all!" I said firmly, and saw her relax at once. "Since I'm not expecting a message from the Prime Minister, I'm sure it doesn't make a particle of difference when I receive this . . . this . . . whatever it is."

I had prompted a weak smile. "Well then, thank you, miss."

She left and I stood—disconcerted—in the middle of the room. Why had Sally been so obsequious? Her natural spunk and verve had evaporated overnight. Overnight. The night in which Geoffrey had been murdered. I guessed the anxiety was catching.

I looked curiously down at the package in my hands, and pulled away the tissue it was wrapped in. It was a thin book, pamphlet sized, whose paper wrappers were beginning to brown at the edges. The title read *Homage to John Dryden: Three Essays on Poetry in the Seventeenth Century* by T. S. Eliot. Inside, the title page said "The Hogarth Press, Tavistock Square, London, W.C. 1 1924."

An unusual and delightful gift, if it was a gift. I opened it to look for a card. A sliver of paper had been tucked into the title page—I unfolded it and looked down.

"GO HOME" the paper said in large block letters. This time I didn't hesitate—I took the book and paper *and* my fright to Michael.

17

"It was an accident," Gamble said.

"Accident?"

"Yes. When we confronted him, he admitted he knew. We tried to bring him along, but he resisted."

"What kind of accident would crush his skull?"

"He started to shout. Philip only meant to stun him."

"Philip. Philip Atherton?"

"Yes. He just planned to tap him, so we could tie him up . . . but the old man lunged at us."

"Lunged at you. Geoffrey . . . " Edmund Littell sat deep in a chair, his arm dangling over its edge. A pool of lamplight lit the gray in his hair.

Gamble was silent.

Finally Littell said, "You needn't stand there. No one can bring him back."

Gamble turned.

"But Keith . . . "

"Sir?"

"Watch yourself. No one is indispensable."

No one but you—or so you think, Gamble said to himself.

He was at the door when Littell called again. "What was Geoffrey doing in the church?"

"When we came in he was kneeling," Gamble answered. "Praying."

18

Geoffrey's funeral was held the next day in the parish church while the Saxon chapel sat padlocked and empty at the end of the lane. It was raining and people clumped together in damp pairs—Sir Edmund and Benson, Lily and David, Michael and I. Neighbors supported Mrs. Tierney.

For some reason I thought the cortege would include a carriage and a horse like the one Dylan Thomas wrote about:

> "Windshake of sailshaped ears, muffle-toed tap
> Tap happily of one peg in the thick
> Grave's foot . . . "

but it was a dove-gray hearse which deposited Geoffrey's casket and later bore it away for cremation.

The vicar looked old enough to have shepherded his flock through the war as well as the tribulations of everyday life. He was a man used to grief, but still read from the Book with ineffable sadness. He and Geoffrey must have been friends and confidants.

Outside, the rain slanted off the gravestones and the churchyard was pungent with woodsmoke drifting up from the village. At the last moment Lily reached out and placed a white rose on the casket, then turned her face into David's shoulder.

After the hearse had departed, there seemed nothing to say. Mrs. Tierney and her neighbors left quietly, and David led Lily away. Sir Edmund started down the steps, then said something to Benson and went back inside the church. Michael and I began to walk across the driveway and were nearly to the car when Superintendent Whitelaw moved out from a hedge which had been screening him. He was carrying a huge umbrella which made him look remarkably like a neighboring oak.

"A sad occasion," he said.

Michael relaxed the hand which had tightened on my elbow. "You took us by surprise, Superintendent. We didn't see you in the church."

"I was there. In the back." The three of us stood silent under the dripping leaves. Then he added, "I suppose you think I came to catch the culprit."

"Not exactly . . . "

"No chance of that in this group. No, I came to see the victim. I always do, you know . . . attend the funeral. There's something about viewing the finality of death which gives an edge to the hunt."

He stood immobile for another moment, then put down his umbrella. "Well. Going back to the house, are you?"

"Yes we are," Michael answered, "and we'd like to talk to you."

"We? Both of you?"

"Yes, both of us. Whenever you're free."

"I'll be in the study. Come in whenever you like."

In the car I succumbed to some flutterings of doubt. "I must say I'm glad we're doing this together. I don't know how Whitelaw will react to what I have to tell him."

"He'll react normally . . . methodically," Michael said. "You're not hallucinating, after all. It happened and we have the proof." He patted the breast pocket where the "go home" note resided.

"But someone searching my room . . . then the men in the garden . . . now the note. Won't it all seem a bit much?"

"More reason to tell him every detail. He has to know what's going on. Look Elizabeth," he turned his head a fraction from the wheel and his voice deepened, "are you prepared to accept the responsibility for *not* telling him?" Without waiting for a reply, he added, "I know you don't want to seem . . . overimaginative . . . but that's not important now. Facts are facts and we have to deal with them."

Deal with the facts and deal with life. Of course. Michael made it sound so simple, but he'd gone through a lot to win that certainty. Now it was my turn. I had to face the fact that Langley was more cloister than career—a cloister from which I could safely view all those involved with life. People who didn't worry about appearances, but barged ahead with the job at hand. Right *then*—that minute—I got sick of dancing around the edges. I would dare, I decided, and try. And have it all—the pain as well as the pleasure.

Twenty minutes later the facts had been laid before the Superintendent, who sat drumming the same fingers on the same desk top. He had made the telling easy, quickly grasping the essentials. He hadn't thought my worry about the misplaced scarf excessive—"observant" was the term he used. He'd spread the note out flat before him, studied it, then used a small, pincer-like object to ease it into a glassine envelope. "It's had considerable handling, so it probably won't tell us much," he commented, "but we'll look it over anyway."

It was the men in the garden who puzzled him. "There were three of them, you say?"

"Yes, Superintendent. It was dark, of course, but I clearly saw three."

"And they were carrying long objects?"

"Yes."

"Could you tell the dimensions of the objects?"

"Not in that light—no."

"I see." He sat thinking for a moment. Then he asked, "*How* did they carry them, Miss Kendall?"

"How?"

"In their arms . . . over their shoulders?"

"Oh. Under their arms, I think."

He had no reply to this, but simply sat staring at me—*through* me, really—as if I weren't there at all. Finally he shook himself.

"Well. So much for that." He stood. "I'm glad you came forward with this information, Miss Kendall. It may be of some help to us."

Michael eyed him with some asperity. "What do you make of all this, Superintendent?"

"Hard to tell," Whitelaw responded blandly. "Hard to tell, Mr. Grandville. We'll have to see."

"Really, Superintendent, that's the kind of answer one gives to an eight-year-old. Even if you can't offer an official judgment, surely you've come to some private conclusions."

"Conclusions?" Whitelaw said sharply. "I don't indulge myself in such luxuries. It's premature to even use the term 'conclusion' . . . unless you want to equate it with guesswork. Which," he added pointedly, "I never do."

He turned his attention to me. "Our forensic crew has finished with Dr. Trehane's cottage, Miss Kendall . . . " There was a smart rap at the door, and Whitelaw's aide Sergeant McGowan came in. "Excuse me."

McGowan leaned down and whispered to the Superintendent. I saw his face change.

"When?"

"Just this morning, sir. In Cadogan Lane."

Whitelaw was obviously disturbed. "All right, McGowan. Wait here, will you?"

"Something the matter, Superintendent?" Michael asked.

"Yes, Mr. Grandville. Our Secretary of Defense Quentin Cooper was killed this morning . . . by a bomb that went off in his car."

"The IRA?"

"We don't know yet."

"I'm sorry . . . "

"So am I. I met him once. A good, hardworking man. Blotted out in seconds." There was quiet rage in Whitelaw's voice.

I murmured, "I'm so sorry . . . . "

He recovered quickly. "Life goes on, Miss Kendall, and you are my immediate concern. As I was saying, we've finished with the cottage . . . searched and taken fingerprints and all that. What we haven't dealt with . . . can't deal with really . . . are his papers. As you may have noticed when you were at the cottage, there are quite a few on his desk."

"I believe Geoffrey was working on an article. He had just finished the research for it."

"Some of the papers seem to be routine notes, but others are in Latin and Old English," he continued. "We aren't equipped to evaluate them . . . to decide which might aid our investigation and which are valuable for their own sake and should be preserved. I was wondering if you would do that for us."

"But I'm not a language expert, Superintendent."

"I understand that. We need someone who will loosely sort the papers out . . . divide them into appropriate categories . . . and bring to our attention anything which seems significant."

He had placed no particular emphasis on the last few words, but their meaning was clear enough. "Are you saying you want me to sift them for clues?" I asked.

Whitelaw sighed. "I'm saying that it would be preferable to have someone who knew Dr. Trehane and has regard for his papers look through them. We *could* pack them all up and send them to an expert in London, but something might get lost in the shuffle. Time would be lost, too. I'm not suggesting that yours would be the definitive examination of the papers, Miss Kendall, but just now it would be helpful if you'd take a look."

I'd seen a few of Geoffrey's notes—they were written in his crabbed but fastidious script. I hated the thought of some constable stuffing them into a briefcase. "All right, Superintendent, I'll try."

"Will you go now, Miss Kendall? Sergeant McGowan can get you a car."

"Just a minute." Michael got up and walked forward so he was leaning—tautly—against the desk. "There's something we haven't discussed. What about Elizabeth's safety?"

"McGowan will stay with her," Whitelaw replied. "She should be perfectly safe."

Michael pointed to the note in the glassine pouch. "You don't think that's a threat?"

"It's been my experience that people who write such notes are no great threat to anyone. There are exceptions, of course, but then the language used is far more hostile. We will speak to Sally to try to pin down when the note was left."

"Is it your view, then," Michael gave full weight to the words, "that Elizabeth is *not* in danger?"

Whitelaw seemed to be considering some elaborate reply, but then said simply and patiently, "As today's events have shown, we are in mortal danger every moment of our lives. I don't think you need be worried about Miss Kendall today . . . and we will deal with each day as it comes along."

He glanced at me. "Are you ready?"

"Yes."

"Good. Here is the key. McGowan will show you to the car. I

need him for a bit, but he'll be along directly. The cottage phone is still in order and I'll call you in an hour or two."

The car was a snappy blue Cortina, and Michael drove part-way with me. "Let me off at the crossroad. I can walk the mile to the hill."

The crew had been trotted past the Superintendent, then cleared for work. "Ian's actor is up there now," Michael said. "We'll wind up tomorrow and everyone can go back to London. Ian and the crew, that is," he added. "I'm staying here with you."

"Oh Michael," I protested, "won't that hold you up?"

"I'm not as noble as I sound. The film has to be processed . . . that should take a few days."

Say it, I thought to myself. Say what you *feel.*

"I'm glad you're staying, Michael. It's good to have you with me . . . to have you near."

"Stop the car." He tapped the wheel.

"What?"

"Pull over."

I did and Michael took me in his arms. I closed my eyes and he kissed me. I felt myself succumbing—reeling backwards into a void where his strength and warmth were the constants. My own hands went around his neck, ran distractedly over his jacket. Tweed and sinew pinned me here, but my head was in flight, soaring away. Something dissolved inside me—the pent-up grief of my famished heart—and I cried aloud.

When we parted, Michael stared across and commanded, "Say it again."

"Say what?"

"That part about wanting me near."

I laughed.

"I want to hear it again," he persisted, deadpan. "Tell me you feel cherished, adored, treasured, transported . . . "

"Try 'secure,' " I said.

"My presence makes you feel *secure?*"

"Yes."

"Well, it shouldn't," Michael said. And he smiled—not his cautious, latter-day smile but the beamish, infectious, mischievous grin of nine years before, when we walked through the streets of Manhattan together.

19

My spirits skittered skyward and the buoyancy lasted until I'd parked the car and let myself into Geoffrey's cottage. Its interior echoed the drizzle outside: it was cold and the furniture felt miserably damp to the touch. Strange. Geoffrey was hardly gone, yet the cottage had taken on the disheartened air of a place long abandoned.

I switched on the heat and waited for the burner to start, then took off my coat. The scarred surface of Geoffrey's big desk was virtually hidden by papers and books. I sat in the Victorian bobbin-turned piece which served as his desk chair and fingered its varnished rungs. Its tartan cushion was worn threadbare, but the chair was comfortable—like an old chum.

I saw rather quickly that the papers were already grouped into categories. There were maps of Thorn Hill and topographical references to manor and parish, the history of the old Priory, medieval descriptions of the village and church, and several volumes on underground chambers and burial mounds. These intrigued me. Had Geoffrey thought there might be treasure buried nearby? McGowan came in, pointed to a corner couch in lieu of conversation, and lowered himself into it—apparently intent on not disturbing me. I settled down myself and began to read.

Outside the sky cleared and the afternoon progressed. I was aware of distant traffic and some carousing as children came home from school but otherwise—for a village house—the place was idyllically private. Geoffrey had preferred a rustic landscape so his neighbors were obscured by a barrier of shrubs, and a high garden wall insulated the rear of the cottage. I read on and on, sorting further as I went along, getting up periodically to massage the stiffness from the back of my neck, exchange words with the Sergeant, and blink at the sun—which had emerged only long enough to fade into the hillside again.

Once the phone rang—it was the Superintendent inquiring about my progress. The hours passed and the desk top altered, as some stacks diminished and others increased. By the time I reached over to turn on a light, four neat piles of material ranged across the back of the desk and another much smaller pile—culled from the rest—sat before me.

Then the phone rang again. A man's voice, vaguely familiar, asked for McGowan.

He took the phone. "Mickle? What? Well, speak up man. Ah . . . never mind. Tell him I'm coming. Bad connection," he added testily to me, "but the gist is that I'm wanted. Be right back."

He left the room and I heard him walking overhead—then he reappeared to check the downstairs windows. Satisfied, he took my arm. "Miss Kendall, you are to lock this door behind me. Don't open it for anyone but me. Mind you . . . no one else. And don't leave the cottage."

"Yes, Sergeant," I said demurely.

He did not look amused. "You're not going to be skittish, are you?"

"No, Sergeant."

"Very well, I'm going. I want to hear the lock turn."

The car drove away. I went back to the desk and stared at the ample depression McGowan had left on the couch; his absence made me uneasy but there was work to be done.

I pulled forward the smallest pile of papers and began to scrutinize each note. Geoffrey had apparently been basing his pamphlet on some new facts he'd found at the Bodleian Library, facts which had emerged from a twelfth-century manuscript on Thorn Hill. The manuscript had been in Latin, of course, and so were his transcripts—I had to rummage through several bookcases to find a Latin dictionary. It was musty and huge—I huffed and puffed a bit getting it back to the desk—but the effort was worth it. I examined the transcript and there it was—"collis spineus"—Thorn Hill. And there was another notation: "Et est ad hunc diem eo loco Ecclesiola . . ." which translated into "to this day at that place there exists a little Church . . ."

So the Saxon chapel had been sufficiently well known in the twelfth century to be chronicled by scholars. The manuscript also referred to a Priory which had been built later. The monastery itself had been destroyed—either by the Danes or the English—but apparently some of the Priory buildings survived. The scholars went on to describe the lives of the monks and the devotion which helped them endure many hardships. They had built a series of artificial caves beneath the Priory, in which they took refuge in times of attack. The caves had provided safe haven for years, but finally the barbarians had prevailed. In my mind's eye I could see the monks fleeing to the woods behind the church, their cassocks flying, pursued by the pillagers and destroyers—the villains of that time and still the hardiest breed.

Enough. I'd done enough reading, my feet were like ice, and I realized I hadn't a thing to eat all day. I went out to the kitchen and found it spotless. Mrs. Tierney must have carefully washed up before walking the lanes in search of Geoffrey. I made myself some sugared tea and bread-and-butter squares. A nursery supper, but the setting had been stripped of its innocence.

I ate my bread and butter slowly at the oilcloth-covered kitchen table. I knew it was all the food I'd have for hours—and I also knew I was putting off tackling the papers again. A little voice had been nattering at me all afternoon, reminding me of the "something" Geoffrey had found. Was that "something" being shuffled through my fingers now?

I was just about to pick up my plate when there was a little noise outside. A clink—like two bottles being knocked together. I walked into the sitting room, but all was quiet. Undisturbed. Back in the kitchen a few moments later, I'd just finished rinsing the utensils when I heard the sound again. This time it was a little louder—pebbles against glass. A neighborhood child out for an evening prank?

Geoffrey's cottage had been built in a "two-cell" plan: sitting room and kitchen side by side downstairs, and two bedrooms up. The kitchen in which I was standing was in the left "cell" and the staircase to the upper floor was at its rear. Since the wind had risen I thought the sound could be a tree branch hitting a window upstairs. I went up to look. The two little bedrooms were eider-downed nests—between them Geoffrey had constructed a tiny bath. All three had windows which were clear of trees.

Back in the sitting room, I went to the desk and tried to focus on the papers. Now every twig which the wind propelled crashed on my consciousness. I shivered. The far reaches of the room were shadowy, gloomy. Gloom. The way to fix that was to have more light. I began turning on lamps, moving some to the corners. It helped. I stepped back to view the cheery glow and my foot crunched on something underneath. Picking it up from the floor was automatic—I rubbed the material—and cried out. Glass. The sliver had cut deep into my finger and the blood was oozing. I used a paper tissue to stop the flow, then bent over the glass on the floor. There was quite a lot of it, tiny bits but also shards.

I checked the sitting-room window and found that the bottom-right pane had been shattered. It had been tapped first—the cracks radiated out to the sash—then poked completely through with something sharp and heavy. It must have happened when I was upstairs, just a few minutes ago. This was no prank—someone had quite deliberately broken the window. I stood there, staring at the fragments glittering on the floor. What did it mean? At that moment I heard a noise in the kitchen, a louder noise—no tinkle, but thud. One thud—then a tattoo of them.

My first reaction was mindless and paralyzing panic. Then I moved to the phone. The Superintendent and Michael were, after all, only minutes away. I picked up the receiver, kept one eye fixed on the window, dialed, and waited. There was no resonance, no buzz. Fear had wiped out my judgment and it took three tries before I knew the telephone was dead. Outside the tattoo halted and I thought I heard a laugh. I sat down.

Stop and think. Whoever was out there could get in if they wanted to—they had the implements and certainly the muscle. For the moment, they were just trying to frighten me. But why?

I walked to the door and pressed my ear against it. All seemed quiet, so I stuck my head out and found the lane was clear. Just then something exploded into the room, shattering the window completely. A rock—hefty, jagged, and brutish—lay on the hooked hearth rug. I heard the laugh again. The snicker. It made me angry—terribly angry—and in my fury, the panic cleared. If it was games they wanted to play, I'd oblige them. I picked up my purse and crammed the smallest pile of Geoffrey's papers into it.

The kitchen light was still on and its counter drawers held a full assortment of cutlery. I chose a boning knife—viciously honed—and a cleaver, plus an iron poker from the kitchen hearth. As I began climbing the stairs there was a great clamor from the sitting room—one crash, then another and another. The windows—all the windows—were being systematically broken. I forced myself to walk upstairs slowly, one step at a time, thinking of Miss Langley and the contempt she would have for these animals. I'd not gratify them by fleeing or collapsing in a craven heap.

Upstairs I picked a bedroom and—panting and shoving—pushed all of its furniture against the door. Surrounded by my arsenal of cleaver-poker-knife I then sat down to wait. As I did, the pounding on the door began again—this time great, thunderous, wood-splitting blows.

20

I don't know how long I sat there listening to those terrible blows. They hammered away with such regularity that I thought the door would surely be split apart, and they became such an assault on my psyche that—although sitting bolt upright—I simply blanked out.

After what seemed like forever, I realized they'd stopped—not tapered off, or dwindled, but stopped abruptly. I was aware first of the silence, then of my blinding headache, then of people running through the lower floor. Had the door been broken down? There was a commotion in the kitchen and shouts—then someone was bounding up the stairs. I picked up the poker, raised it shakily—and Superintendent Whitelaw burst in. He was followed by two burly men, and between them they swept the piled furniture aside as if bed and bureau had been dollhouse decorations.

I remember thinking how absurd those enormous men looked in that little room—their heads brushing the trellised roses on the wallpapered ceiling—and I felt strangely moved as the Superintendent came toward me. His face was white and strained under the overhead light.

"Miss Kendall!" he exclaimed, taking my face in both hands and turning my head gently from side to side—peering at me—then turning to one of the sergeants and calling brusquely for a doctor.

At that moment there was more noise on the stairs, the sound of someone taking them two at a time. Michael ran in and stopped dead in his tracks when he saw me.

"Elizabeth! My God, Elizabeth! Where are you hurt?"

"Hurt?" I made an effort to sound composed, but the word was really a croak. "I'm not hurt at all."

"Look." Michael pulled a round mirror from a nail on the wall. I stared at my reflection in amazement. Smudges of blood—caking now—trailed across my face and I saw that the front of my raincoat was patterned in umber blotches. I *was* hurting, I realized—there was an ache somewhere in my hand. Then I understood.

"Oh, my finger!" I said, holding it up.

This was echoed by a baritone chorus: "Finger?"

"I cut it on the glass downstairs," I answered, "and the bleeding must have started again."

Michael and the Superintendent appeared to fold inside themselves, drooping with relief, and after a prolonged stare one of the stolid sergeants left. He was back a minute later with a wet towel which he none-too-gently used on my face, wiping the blood away in rotary sweeps which made my cheeks sting.

Cleaned up, I was ushered downstairs where McGowan was seated in a kitchen chair, looking dazed and gingerly probing his scalp.

"He was found in a ditch," Whitelaw said shortly. "When did he leave you?"

"In the late afternoon, Superintendent. Soon after Mickle called."

"Mickle never called . . . McGowan got caught." There wasn't much sympathy in Whitelaw's voice. "So much for precautions. Let's go."

From the car the cottage looked ravaged—broken windows agape, the front door hanging open, a troop of men moving inside. First Geoffrey, now this. I was heartsick. What could that gentle academic have done to drive anyone to that pitch of destruction?

Part of the motive was made clear to me the following day. Sally had just taken away my coat to be sponged when McGowan appeared. He had either recovered quickly or was trying to redeem himself in spite of his wounds: his aspect was rueful, but businesslike.

"Miss Kendall, Superintendent Whitelaw would like to know what papers you took from the cottage."

"Just these," I pulled them from the purse and explained the sorting-out. "The rest I left on the desk."

"The rest?"

"The papers I didn't think were particularly important."

"They're gone now, miss."

"Gone!"

"The desk was as clean as a whistle when we started our look-around. The Superintendent hoped you had salvaged something. He asked me to tell you to take good care of any papers you have until he gets back. The Superintendent is in London today, miss," he added, making Whitelaw sound like a store manager gone to view the prime branch. He made a few perfunctory inquiries about my health, and left.

I spent the next hour poking around my room, tying my books together and packing the script ingredients. I had no idea what I'd use these for, but habits die hard: trimly indexed files were fixtures of my secondhand life. Once or twice, for a breath of fresh air, I walked to the window. The view was unchanged—pastoral and serene—the students plodding across the hill and the tent gently flapping. After the agitation of the night before, the scene seemed to proceed at slow-motion pace.

When the packing was done, I sat aimlessly at the edge of the bed. Officially I was "resting," but I didn't think I could spend my day lounging. Besides, there were now *two* voices nagging at me. The more querulous one was asking why Geoffrey's cottage had been rifled. Who were the intruders? Now I knew they'd been bent upon stealing what lay on Geoffrey's desk. But why?

The other voice was the same one which had been badgering me the day before. Everything has been picked apart, it said, except the papers beneath your hand—those you selected wheat-from-chaff. What Geoffrey wanted you to know—to see—must be secreted somewhere among them. You must look *now!* Finally I could stand it no longer, and spread everything out on the dressing table.

There seemed to be no surprises. I'd simply set aside any item—map, manuscript, or note—which couldn't be evaluated at first glance. I pared down again and mulled over what remained. There were several pages in Geoffrey's hand on Pictish souterrains—he'd underlined one sentence which described subterranean passages eighty feet long. There was a batch of old maps with some Thorn Hill references circled and—surprisingly for Geoffrey—a rather elaborate doodle. It repeated the phrase "mark the baeddle" in a background of interwoven Celtic spirals, knots, and scrolls.

Mark the baeddle. "Baeddle" was Old English for monster—hence "bad"—so the doodle meant "observe the monster." But which monster? Not an actual one, surely; there were no Nessies lurking in the south of England. Perhaps Geoffrey had just copied a random phrase—a word combination which pleased him. The doodle was fanciful enough; the scrolls and spirals whirled around the script. I decided Geoffrey had done it for relaxation—just to rest the mind—and thought of asking Whitelaw if I might have the scrap eventually. A fragment of Geoffrey to keep for myself when—and if—the murder was resolved.

The notes on the souterrains explained that the majority were found in Scotland and Ireland, but that examples of underground tunnels could be found as far south as west Cornwall. Geoffrey's supposition was that the practice of building souterrains had spread from south to north along Britain's Atlantic coast. He seemed to be fascinated by their construction—paved floors and dry-stone walls which were able to carry heavy slab roofs at heights of six feet or more.

There were three maps and all looked interesting. One was contemporary, one dated 1910, and the last printed—I judged—in the mid-1800s. It was remarkable how little the village had changed through the years. There were more "lanes" than "streets" on the earlier maps, but otherwise the village had remained compact, nestled between the dual influence of church and manor. A hundred years ago the manor had commanded the same expanse of acreage and the church—or churches—punctuated the village's northern boundaries.

I examined the tiny squares Geoffrey had circled behind the Saxon chapel. These only appeared on the earliest map and had to be the medieval stone outbuildings. There was nothing else in that lane so close to the little church. The ancient Priory had been near that spot, too. I felt a sudden, gripping stir of excitement. Could the outbuildings really be the Priory remains? Was that Geoffrey's discovery?

It fitted. Geoffrey had gone to Oxford and the Bodleian Library there to research his historical pamphlet. In the course of that research he'd learned that the two outbuildings were not part of the charnel house—not vaults for the dead—but actually part of the Priory which had been sacked and destroyed by barbarians. In the minds of the villagers the outbuildings had always been linked to the Saxon chapel—the three lumped together through the centuries and the Priory long forgotten. The archeological excitement generated by Sir Edmund's grandfather had all been focused on the church, and the outbuildings left to crumble at the rear of the chapel garden.

But why was the discovery so significant? Why did Geoffrey feel he must keep it secret at all cost? Why would someone feel so threatened by it that a vicious raid was staged? Could it have caused his murder? The questions swirled through my mind, maddening and unanswerable.

I tried to apply the principles of examination which I taught in the Langley classrooms. Two ancient buildings had been found to be older than supposed. That was the sum of it. No world-shaking revelation sat in the village—just two decrepit structures with an elevated pedigree.

Then something clicked—all those notes on the souterrains. I shuffled the papers—searching—and found the passages on the monks. When threatened, they had hidden in artificial caves beneath the Priory. Weren't souterrains and caves the same? I sat back and thought. *Of course.* What Geoffrey had actually found was a series of underground tunnels, dating back to a primitive time, still in existence at Thorn Hill. That was the fact which had made him sound so tremulous on the phone and which—I realized when I looked down—was making my own hands shake.

I put the paper flat on the desk and smoothed its bent edges, my mind skimming the possibilities. Suppose—just suppose—that Geoffrey had found something *inside* the caves. Thoughts of actual treasure seemed a juvenile dream, but he had once spoken of such legends persisting. What if Geoffrey had stumbled on something really valuable—something coveted? Pectoral crosses on gold cloisonné, jeweled chalices, huge silver bowls with enameled escutcheons—all had been twentieth-century finds in Britain, pulled from an assortment of burial places.

And many had been killed for much less.

21

"Where is he?" Sidney Bullock demanded.

"I told you, he's busy," Benson said.

"Not too busy to meet with scoundrels like Baker, I'm sure. I must talk to him."

"I'm sorry. He wasn't expecting you."

Gamble stood in the doorway. "None of us were. You were stupid to come here."

"How dare you speak to me . . . "

"Somebody better. Suppose someone's seen you. What's the matter with you? Can't you think of those things?"

"Perhaps we could give him a message," Benson added.

Bullock looked from one to the other. "Yes. Tell him this. There'll be no demonstration until we talk face-to-face. There'll be no demonstration which uses grenades. He must choose between Baker . . . and me.

"Give him that message," Bullock said, walking out the front door.

22

I was deep in tumultuous thought when Sally knocked and came in, carrying my raincoat and calling out, "Luncheon, miss."

Luncheon. The word had a tearoom ring and I remembered those women on Marylebone Street—how many days ago? They would have had luncheon as an afternoon treat, bits of salad and slivers of sandwiches, the worldwide shopper's ritual. I'd seen those women in Boston too—coursing back to Beacon Hill with parcels from Bonwit's and Jordan Marsh—sleek, secure women going home for the predinner cocktail. I'd thought myself indifferent to them but then, back at Langley, they would stride in my memory—glossy hair flying, the good tweed barely showing beneath the plump furs. It had taken me years to acknowledge that I wasn't indifferent at all, that what I felt was gnawing jealousy.

"I'm not very hungry, Sally," I said.

She looked really distressed. "I think you should eat something, miss. You've had a shock."

"Feed up the trauma? I don't think that's medically sound, but all right. I'll go down." On the staircase I realized eating was wise after all. I'd just decided I would look for Geoffrey's caves and had the feeling that would take both clear head and strong body.

I didn't plan to tell Michael. He would flatly forbid me to go, then notify Sergeant McGowan. If the caves *did* exist, McGowan would muck them up good, trundling through with his team of experts. Experts they were—in homicide—but in the Superintendent's absence they were not likely to cherish archeological details. And those details were the reason I was going—not to probe into murder, but to preserve the fruits of Geoffrey's scholarship.

In the hall I saw a glowering Marsden slam out the front door, then heard his estate jeep pulling away. I'd be spared his company, and that was a boon. On the long buffet in the dining room, lunch was arranged on a white linen runner beside some fat chrysanthemums sitting in a Staffordshire jug. David stood at one end, forking cutlets onto his plate. He looked a bit startled to see me.

"I was told you'd be in bed today."

"Couldn't bear the idea. Besides, I feel fine."

"You're sure?" David's eyes flickered quickly, an examining glance. Looking for bruises, it seemed.

"The nerves are a bit jangled, but otherwise I'm all right. Really. No reason to languish upstairs."

"At least let me help you with that." He took my plate and we sat at the table.

We ate silently for a few moments, then David said, "I'm leaving tomorrow, Elizabeth. I must get back to my play."

"Oh? I hope we see you in London."

"I'm sure you will." He wiped his lips, took a sip of water, and looked at me. "You should know that Lily and I are going our separate ways. I had to stay long enough to see her through the funeral. She's better now, I think."

Word for word, David then justified Michael's prediction. "Elizabeth, I can't be all things to her. Lover-brother-father-*foot-*

man. No man can do all she wants . . . give her all she needs. I can stay and be consumed, or walk away now. I'm walking." He paused. "I guess that sounds rotten."

"You're a playwright, David, not Lily's keeper. I'm sorry for her, but after all you must . . . " I stopped. Keith Gamble stood in the doorway, his hands in his blue blazer pockets, smiling jauntily at us both.

"Well, this is a treat. I'd been quite put out at the idea of eating alone, but this is fine. Cozy."

David's face shuttered abruptly. He pushed his plate to one side and rose. "I'll see you, Elizabeth," he murmured, and left.

Gamble seemed indifferent to his departure. "Just the two of us, I see, Miss Kendall. Be with you in a minute." He jiggled his plate along the buffet, humming over the sauceboats, then plunked down at the table. His face assumed a look of strained solicitude.

"I'm so glad to see you've recovered from your experience last night. Trying for you, I'm sure."

"Frightening, yes. But I'm all right now."

"Have the police any idea who might be responsible?"

"I can't say. I haven't seen Superintendent Whitelaw today. He left for London this morning."

"Ah. Well, I trust they'll get it sorted out in time. Really, the episode didn't surprise me."

"What?"

"Sitting ducks," he continued blandly. "That's what these empty cottages are. Word gets around that Trehane is dead . . . the news spreads to the town. There are men at a pub, a few drinks are consumed, and someone says the old boy must have had valuable stuff. They decide to make an inspection."

"They would have to be ghouls."

"Times have changed, Miss Kendall. One can't even be sure of the neighboring farmer . . . "

I stood up very quickly. "You must excuse me. I have some work to do."

In the hall I took several deep breaths. It was bliss to be out of the room. That granite jaw, the suede-textured blond hair, the voice prattling on, those specious conclusions—the man was impossible.

I ran quickly up to my room, pulled on my raincoat, and began stuffing the pockets with supplies for my adventure: car keys, a flashlight, and my little camera—in case I found wall inscriptions worth photographing. They all spoiled my raincoat's freshly pressed symmetry, but a purse would be an encumbrance.

As a precaution, I left a note on my mirror for Sally. "Gone fishing" was what I was tempted to write—it was accurate enough. Instead I scribbled "Gone exploring. Back by 6," which gave a time framework if I were detained. Tucking the note in the mirror frame, I stared at myself and recalled how I'd looked in the mirror Michael had held. The blood. I had fingered my face and my clothes in absolute panic—not feeling or seeing—as if engaged in some primitive rote.

I was not frightened now, though, and I wanted to go. If there were souterrains—caves—they might only provide a scholarly footnote in history books. But the credit would accrue to Geoffrey, and even minor glories would give punctuation to the life he'd been so wistful about.

I parked the Cortina deep beneath the trees at the end of the church lane; no point in attracting attention. The simple garden which encircled the Saxon chapel ended at that point, the rest of the grounds were overgrown and scruffy, and a narrow, well-trodden path led to the outbuildings. I remembered Geoffrey saying that one of the buildings was used to store stones of various periods which had been found buried nearby. These would be sorted out and any with Saxon decoration used to make a stone altar to replace the chapel's wooden one. Geoffrey had been amused at the amazing fit of some of the stones. He felt they had probably been part of an original altar and had been "borrowed" by ancient farmers for their own use.

The outbuildings stood about fifty feet apart. They had been built in plain, square shapes, almost boxlike except for the peak at the roof. According to Geoffrey's notes the Priory had existed in 1001, which is probably why the outbuildings looked so nondescript—too late for the peak of excellent Saxon stonework, too early for Norman solidarity. I guessed they had been used as functional dormitories for the lesser monks, the "privates" of this religious order. The better quarters would have belonged to the abbot—grander, more spacious dwellings, logical targets for the invaders and enemies of the church. These hadn't survived. There was a certain brutal simplicity in that object lesson, I thought.

The first outbuilding—the one nearest the lane—was empty and in very poor shape. Parts of the roof opened to the sky, there was debris strewn about and a general air of decay. I walked down the track to the second and found it much sturdier. The roof seemed to be whole and the wooden door worked on its rusting hinges. I pulled it open and stepped over the hill.

It was dim inside—my eyes took a minute or two to adjust. Then I saw the interior was bare except for the stones, which were grouped in orderly piles at the rear third of the room. Everything looked surprisingly swept up and tidy—the archeological touch. I stood there, floundering a bit. Where to begin? Everything seemed so orderly—or ordinary. What had I expected then—a yawning chasm billboarded by a neon sign? If a tunnel entrance had escaped the notice of those assembling the stones, it would surely not present itself easily to *me.*

I examined the walls, but that took just a moment. Through the chinks in the mortar I could see bits of sunshine outside; the walls were fortress-like by modern standards, but really too thin for concealment. I began going over the floor, inch by inch. Its pavement was riddled with cracks and holes but seemed solid enough and I began wondering. Could the monks have built the tunnel entrance outside? The plot would have been heavily wooded then—a thick grove perhaps just a few steps away. Since the churchyard had often been used as a dumping ground, the entrance would be refuse-filled and forgotten. Musing, I walked over to the stones.

They were rough and cool to the touch, but not slimy. I leaned against one pile experimentally—it did not budge. If the stones were so heavy, how had they been moved there and placed in alignment? I looked at the floor near the front of the piles. The dust there was talcum-fine; there were no ground chips or deep scrapes. Odd. Geoffrey had mentioned that the stones were collected continually—but I felt these had been put in place some time ago, and then the room neatly swept.

I worked my way around to the rear row of stones, those next to the wall. There I found the essential tool—a huge, pincer-like object leaning against the wall. It looked almost exactly like the turn-of-the-century ice tongs I'd seen in old New England almanacs. I fingered the pincers. This was a much heavier, a much coarser tool; it looked as if it would bite deeply into the stones that it grabbed. It would probably need expert handling; misuse might mar the stone decoration.

I pulled out my flashlight, cast it over the floor, and found it as tidy as elsewhere. The end stone was exceptionally large, at least five feet high by three feet deep, and it looked more abused that the others. Its sides were gored by the pincers, as if the tool had been applied again and again. If the stone had been shifted often, why wasn't there more debris on the floor? I put my flashlight down, gingerly picked up the pincers, and managed a clumsy grasp of the stone. I pulled—and then gasped. The whole stone had shifted.

Shifted at least a foot with almost no effort; it seemed like some conjurer's sleight-of-hand trick. I pulled again harder and this time it barreled right up to my cheek. I put the pincers aside and kneeled, running the torch along the floor. The stone seemed elevated, *was* elevated just a few inches; I could run my hand beneath it. It sat on a platform—a steel platform, I judged, with ball-bearing wheels.

Disdaining the pincers, I pulled the stone forward again—its bulk slid like a mound of papier-mâché. There was something behind it. Another pull and the stone was free of the pile. What I saw made me step back in shock. I was faced by a wooden frame which was camouflaged all around by the rest of the rocks. Peering ahead, I saw the frame formed an entryway—and the entryway led to a flight of stairs, going down.

The tunnel entrance. It had to be. I snatched up the flashlight again and moved forward, ducking my head to clear the frame. The steps were perilously steep and badly worn at the edges: my one free hand clawed at the wall for support. Seven-eight-nine steps down and I was standing at the bottom; standing upright but with barely an inch to spare. The souterrain stretched along beyond the beam of my flashlight and I suddenly faltered. I could see the faint light from the building above—in front of me there was pitch darkness. Moving ahead would be losing contact with the outside world, entering a dungeon of earth. I felt a shaft of pure fear as the old superstitions stirred—tombs, bats, and burials.

Then I thought—rubbish. If this was the Priory tunnel it was almost a thousand years old and not likely to crumble the instant I entered it. The rock walls and floor were dry, the air seemed to be circulating, and I felt I could cope with small creatures—however repugnant. Timidity belonged to that other girl—the hesitant, tepid Elizabeth. I got a good grip on my flashlight, and walked on.

I'd moved about thirty paces when the tunnel widened

and—reaching up—I found I could touch the roof only with my fingertips. I was moving into a bigger space. At that point the passage also began to curve, and when I looked I saw total blackness behind. With each step forward, part of my mind measured the distance back to the stairway; I'd met neither threat nor impediment, but each pace took me further away. I wondered, how long could the tunnel be? I went around another bend and had my answer: the main passage continued into the darkness, but a branch sloped to a linteled doorway six feet ahead. Walking through it, I almost tripped over something standing on the floor. My torch found the object—a battery lantern. I picked it up and fiddled with the switch, doubtful that it would work; but it sprung to life suddenly, casting a surprising amount of light in all directions.

I was standing in a chamber—a large chamber, roughly the size of the lounge at Langley. It had the tidy look of the room upstairs, but this place was furnished. There was a high table, rather like a lectern but squarer, in front of the room. Six pairs of benches, diagonally placed, were arranged in rows fanning back from the table. It looked like a classroom. No. It looked like a church. I wondered why I felt chilled at the thought.

I made a brief search of the rest of the chamber, holding the lantern high and casting its beam into all the dark corners. Except for the furniture in its rigid arrangement, the place was completely empty. In spite of my brave intentions, I began to feel desperately uneasy. What was this place? Who worked or worshipped here? Then the frightening question: How would they view a trespasser?

I had a strong instinct to run—to dump the lantern and tear back along the tunnel. But that passed. The strangeness of my surroundings persisted, however. I'd come hoping to discover a Late Saxon refuge marked by remnants of pottery—or perhaps by an inscription carved on a wall. What I'd found was this antiseptic underground chamber, as precise as a stage set, obviously recently used. But by whom?

I walked past the benches to the high square table and saw that it was covered by a piece of green felt. The felt was raised up from the table; there was something solid beneath it. Although I knew there was no one nearby, I found myself looking around the room again. Then I picked up one edge of the felt and slowly—cautiously—lifted the material. There was a cross on the table—not a polished, bejeweled object, but a queer leaden thing.

Its front was engraved. I sat the lantern down on the table and picked up the cross with both hands. Although the lead was dull, it was clean, and the inscription was legible: HIC IACET SEPULTUS INCLITUS REX ARTURIUS IN INSULA AVALONIA.

"Here lies buried the famous King Arthur in the isle of Avalon."

It was the Cross of Arthur I held.

23

Arthur's burial cross. My mind reeled through the dozens of descriptions I'd read of it. In 1190, at Glastonbury Abbey, the monks had found two bodies buried deep in the ground in a hollowed oak. Two-thirds of the coffin held the bones of a man and the other third those of a woman. There was a lock of yellow hair which, when picked up by a monk, fell into dust. The man's thighbone and skull were of gigantic size and bore the marks of many wounds. The wounds had all healed except a great one, which must have been the cause of death.

A leaden cross was fixed to a stone beneath the coffin, with an engraved inscription on its inner face, toward the stone. It marked the grave as King Arthur's and the woman was thought to be Guinevere. The remains had been taken into the church for a proper burial in a marble tomb. The cross was seen again in 1542 by the antiquary Leland, and in 1607 Camden's *Britannia* had included both the inscription and a drawing of the cross. The cross in my hands matched them both.

Even without the memory of the Camden sketch—words which straggled across the surface and the squared letter Cs—I knew the cross was real and not counterfeit. It had the look and the feel of the ages, the worn purity of a venerable object. My hands were trembling as I put the cross down. How had it gotten there? Who was in charge of it? Was this table lectern or altar? Why was the tunnel—and this chamber—kept hidden?

I must leave. Every dictate of self-preservation was pulling me back through the tunnel. There was no more to be found in this room and I hadn't the will to search further. Other passages might trail endlessly—snaky paths through the earth—leading away from the outbuilding entry and the world outside. Whoever belonged here—those who assembled this shrine for the cross—might be back any minute. I didn't want to face them before I knew what their motives were—what had driven them underground.

I stared at the cross; stared at it so long that my head began swimming and, when I raised it, white dots danced across the shadowy walls. Then I thought: Should I take it with me? I had only to reach down, pluck it from the table, then run like the wind.

But that would be foolish. I didn't know what alarms would be raised when the cross was found missing—what the consequences might be. I'd tell the Superintendent; it would be better if he saw everything just as it was. Shakily, I raised my small camera, set it for flash, and took two quick pictures.

Then I carefully replaced the square of green felt, picked up the lantern, and walked to the doorway. Before pressing the lantern switch I looked around the chamber again. The monks must have held services here centuries ago; I could imagine them moving through the timeless rituals. Now a ghostly place, its stark furniture mute, the room harbored other—more threatening—mysteries. I switched off the lantern, placed it on the floor, and made my way back through the tunnel.

Stepping around the last dark bend, I could have cried out in relief at the sight of the stairway ahead. I went up like a shot, not looking behind, and pushed the stone into place. I leaned the pincers against the wall again and flashed my light over the floor to make sure nothing appeared to be disturbed.

Then I walked out into the open air, where even the weeds lining the track seemed magically filigreed, and the trees and blue sky loomed like miracles above.

My books were packed snugly. On my knees on the bedroom floor, I hacked at the twine with a manicure scissors and yanked at the tape impatiently. Finally the paper parted, I pulled out several volumes, and began reading.

Both books covered Arthur thoroughly—as warlord, fifth-century prince, and the source of enduring mythology. With the legends stripped away, the historical facts were skimpy. He was born about 475, fought at the mammoth Battle of Badon in 495, and died with Medraut at Camlann—or "crooked glen"—in 515. The dates, of course, were approximate.

The authors said Arthur may have been the last emperor of Britain, an all-conquering military commander, a mighty ruler who stabilized the government of his people—or played all of these roles. The circumstances of his burial were mysterious and the most powerful traditions implied that one day he would live again. Writing in the twelfth century, Geoffrey of Monmouth had described the fatál battle: "Even the renowned King Arthur himself was wounded deadly and was borne thence unto the island of Avalon . . ." Writing at the same time, William of Malmesbury had said: ". . . the tomb of Arthur is nowhere beheld, whence the ancient ditties fable that he is yet to come."

But Arthur was reputed to be a patron of Glastonbury Abbey and at that time Glastonbury—almost surrounded by marshes and lagoons—was more or less an island in wet weather. Many thought it was the ancient Isle of Avalon. The monks found the grave between two stone pyramids in the abbey churchyard. Reports of the grave and its contents were given by a contemporary chronicler, and by Gerald of Wales, who visited Glastonbury in 1192 and 1193 and saw the bones and the tomb that was built to hold them. The tomb was opened in 1278 for Edward I, who was keeping Easter at Glastonbury with Queen Eleanor. The bones were later transferred to a more elaborate tomb in front of the high altar, where they remained until the time of the English Reformation, when they were dug up, scattered, and lost forever.

There was much scholarly argument about the cross. The inscription was troublesome because it was obviously not contemporary with Arthur's death in the sixth century—the shape of the letters was wrong for that time. Some experts claimed that the 1190 exhumation was a fraud staged by the monks to raise money for the building fund.

So the cross had suffered a long period of ill repute. When the speculation had sifted down through recent research, however, a plausible theory had been offered. Arthur had been buried in the abbey churchyard near a mausoleum which held the body of an important saint. His grave would have been marked by an upright slab or pillar, as was sixth-century custom, probably inscribed in Roman capitals which said the equivalent of "Here lies Arthur."

When Saint Dunstan was Abbot of Glastonbury after 945, he had enclosed the old cemetery with a wall and raised the area, demolishing the mausoleum. Some historians now believed that if there was a monument to Arthur standing nearby, it would have been removed at that time and transferred to the spot the monks had uncovered. The upright slab had been replaced by a lead cross inscribed in tenth-century letters that reflected Arthurian legends which already were widespread: "famous king Arthur" and "the isle of Avalon." This was the cross I had held an hour ago—a cross not of Arthur's time, but one which had lain with his bones and those of his beautiful Guinevere.

It was priceless—the only Arthurian relic still in existence. The tests for dating ancient objects had reached levels of sophistication undreamed of by early archeologists; the century when the cross had been made could be pinpointed and the sequence of Arthur's burials confirmed. It would bring him into focus—rescue him from the uncertainty imposed by the mists of time and the force of legends.

And stir the folklore again. I reread part of a fifteenth-century poem from the Red Book of Bath:

"At Glastonbury on the queer
They made Artourez toumbe there,
And wrote with latyn verse thus
Hic jacet Arthurus, rex quondam, rex futurus."

Arthur, the past and future king. Arthur would reign again—that had been the cry from ancient bard to Tennyson's *Idylls.* The twentieth century had viewed the matter more cynically—until a little tribe of persistent archeologists had uncovered Dark Age traces in areas traditionally linked to the legends.

The cross would make possible Arthur's return—in spirit at least. It would give heart to a Britain struggling with the melancholy problems of a modern time. It would also remind them that generations of heroes had sprung from this single magnificent man—and that there were heroes to come. The cross had that power.

My book said it had been in the hands of a private family in Wells until sometime in the eighteenth century, when it had vanished. I put the book down. Wells was less than thirty miles from Thorn Hill. Had the cross been secreted all those years, passed from hand to hand? More likely it had been dumped on some attic-clearing auction—country-house chattel—and snatched up by someone who recognized it.

I was sure now that Geoffrey had found it—followed the

Bodleian clues, discovered the tunnel, and made the same trip through its serpentine darkness. And though the thought filled me with horror, I admitted what I'd instinctively known the instant I'd picked up the cross: that it had caused Geoffrey's death. There was no other reason for him to be brutally bludgeoned and left on the cold stones of the chapel floor.

I must find Michael and tell him—perhaps there was something we both could do before the Superintendent returned. It was almost dusk; I sped the car past the silent yews and down the road to the village. The streets were virtually empty; the stores were closing and only a few people could be seen walking home. I drove next to Thorn Hill, but there were no vans at its base—just some filming equipment dismantled and already crated, spectral on the darkening slope. At the inn, the manager nodded; the crew had left an hour ago. Mr. Grandville must be somewhere about. The pub was empty, save a few country types. Disappointed, I turned back toward the manor.

My eyes were fixed on the road but my mind reexamined the underground chamber. The questions it posed were insistent. Were the tunnel people a Druid-like sect—a secret cult? Did they worship the cross? I knew that such groups existed in Britain, but the ones I'd seen pictured just pranced around Stonehenge in flowing white robes. They seemed mere eccentrics; not given to violence. I imagined Geoffrey confronted—flailing—smashed. He had been killed without mercy.

I pulled up to the house and sat in the car—drained—repelled by the image. One thing I was certain of: I could not see us facing them, whoever they were, without the Superintendent and his men. Michael and I must go to McGowan. Wearily, I dragged my whole sagging self up the front steps and pushed the bell. There were thuds on the wooden floor inside as someone rushed forward, then the door was flung open. I was amazed to see

Marsden standing there, agitated and breathless. He reached out for me, his fingers biting into my shoulders, and drew me inside asking, "Where have you been?"

At first I just cringed away. I had a clear recollection of that night at the table and the pain he'd inflicted. Then I got angry.

"Take your hands off me."

"Where the hell have you been?"

"If you don't take your hands away," I answered, "I'm going to scream."

"Scream then. You were told not to leave the house."

"Not true. But if I *had* been, it's still none of your business."

"Fool! Don't you see that . . ."

There was a voice down the hall. "What's going on here?" The hands relaxed and then fell as Michael came toward us.

He looked furious. "What do you think you're doing, Marsden?"

"I'm bidding Miss Kendall good-evening," Marsden answered. He tried a smile. "And warning her of things that go bump in the night. See you," he added, and walked out the door.

Michael looked after him. "What was that all about?"

"I don't know. He's some kind of a wild man."

"Rotten brute. If he comes near you again, I'll . . ."

"It's all right, Michael. He just thinks he's my keeper."

"He has some colossal nerve . . ." I put a finger to Michael's lips and he stopped speaking, then started again. "Say, where have you been?"

I opened my mouth to answer, but the question, repeated that way, seemed suddenly funny. I started to laugh, softly and almost apologetically at first, then harder and harder. The fright at the cottage, the stumbling trip through the tunnel, the shock of the cross had all taken their toll.

I laughed until I gasped, until I wept, and Michael watched me. When my sides ached and my breath was spent I stopped, and Michael put an arm around me and led me to the privacy of the telephone niche. I looked up at him, my eyes blurred by tears.

"I'm sorry . . ."

"Best thing you could do. Do you have a handkerchief?"

"Yes . . . here . . . ," I fumbled and found one. "By God, you are a practical man."

"Practical men," he gave me a hug, "make the world go round. Listen, I'm almost afraid to ask, but I would like to know. Where *have* you been?"

"Oh, Michael, I . . ."

"Because I've been looking for you, Beth. I've something shocking to tell you."

24

Lily cowered in a fireplace chair, her knees up to her chin, her hands covering her ears. The smouldering hearth gave off a sour smell. Keith Gamble leaned in, took her wrist, and pulled her hand free.

"You must listen to me."

"Please . . ."

"History will be made . . . is being made . . . and you're part of it."

She moaned, "Please . . ."

"You can't run away, Lily. You have to accept your role. Accept me. That's what your father would wish."

"My father—" she pushed him away—"my father must be insane."

"You're wrong. The plan is brilliant, and it's going to work. He said there'll be a new England for you and your children. He means it, Lily. He'd do anything for you."

Gamble slid his hand under her hair, stroked the back of her neck. "He'd kill for you, Lily."

"Kill?"

"Yes, kill. I thought you'd guessed. He ordered Geoffrey's death."

25

Michael's news *was* shocking enough to cast me into another patch of uncertainty, another dimension of fear. That afternoon the crew had just left when Ian, who planned a few days in Cornwall, asked Michael for a lift to the car-hire garage. They had been driving through the village, chatting, when suddenly Ian stiffened.

"Michael, don't stop, but drive to the end of this row, then turn around and drive back . . . slowly this time."

Mystified, Michael had done so.

"Isn't that Gamble's house?"

Michael had turned his head to view a small structure set off to one side. There was a car in front and two men walking toward it.

"Yes, it is."

"Quick. Look at the man on the left."

He was tall and walked with a peculiar gait. The face looked somewhat familiar, but Michael glanced over and back without much recognition.

"Who . . ."

"I don't think they noticed us. Quickly again now. Turn and drive back . . . oh damn! They're in the car . . . they're leaving."

Michael pulled over and stopped.

"Ian, what's going on?"

"That man. You must know who he is."

"I know I've seen him before, but that's all."

"It's Sidney Bullock."

"Bullock!"

"Yes, indeed. Here at Thorn Hill. The racist M.P. . . . the bigot's delight."

Ian had given Michael a brief lecture on Bullock, who'd begun life as the scion of an old landholding family and had, as an undergraduate in the thirties, joined Oswald Mosley's blackshirt troops, lock-stepping through the London streets. He'd redeemed himself with outstanding wartime service, earned a law degree, and won a seat in Parliament. He was known as an ultraconservative, but his career had proceeded more or less placidly until the early sixties.

"When he began turning up at meetings to protest immigration standards," Ian said. "Bullock uses poverty and unemployment as devices to feed hatred. He's behind a new group of agitators and has been organizing protests for them. Lately the protests have turned into riots.

"His followers call for deportation of all black and Asian immigrants, and the boats they speak about smack of the cattle cars of Germany. There's the smell of the beer hall about him, a shade of the little man with the moustache. There's fear we'll see jackboots and blackshirts in Hyde Park again."

Ian had sunken into sober, rueful silence as Michael proceeded to the garage. He then gave a handshake and got out of the car, but stuck his head through its open window.

"It's the time that baffles me, Michael."

"The time?"

"Time of day. Bullock has such a rotten reputation now that he has to be cagey about his moves. If he *had* to see Gamble—for God knows what reason—one would think he'd come at night. Not in broad daylight. He must have known he'd be seen in this tiny place."

"Not necessarily. It was just a fluke that *we* saw him."

"All the same, it makes me uneasy—Bullock taking those chances. Maybe he's finally gone around the bend."

Now Michael looked as solemn as I imagined Ian had been. "Ian's right. It makes one wonder. What business can Bullock have in Thorn Hill—particularly with Gamble?"

"Something to do with the dig, perhaps? Funding it as a goodwill gesture?"

"According to Ian, he's past the point of goodwill. Even the members of his own party detest him."

"Why do they tolerate him then? Why isn't he ousted?"

"Because of the old political game, Beth. They're afraid of offending his supporters . . . many of them middle class and unhappy about the way Britain is going. Other supporters are rabid Far Right. Ian says there have been a lot of rumblings lately about an immense private army."

"An army?"

"Yes, battalions of armed citizens who first mobilized early in 1974 . . . a bad time for England. There was a state of emergency due to the power shortage and a crippling miners' strike, which was in danger of turning into a General Strike. To prevent a national calamity, thousands of people offered their services to maintain law and order and keep public services going. Reactionaries among them talked of forming a new national government.

"The crisis passed, but the fervor for the new government didn't. Some books and newspapers now say there are a hundred thousand Englishmen, supported by right-wing funds and manipulated by a fascist bloc, ready to march. Ian thinks Bullock is their man in Parliament, their front. He's no mastermind . . . he's not that clever . . . but he can agitate in the highest political circles. Right now that's destructive enough."

I shuddered. "Michael, that's frightening."

"Indeed it is. Bullock should be stopped, and I plan to do my part this evening. I'm going to tell Sir Edmund about Gamble's visitor and, when Whitelaw gets back, drop the word to him as well. I'm sure Sir Edmund will want to ask Gamble some questions about his new friend. Whitelaw too. I can't see . . ."

Michael stepped back and looked at me narrowly. "You're so pale, Beth. What a fool I am. This isn't the time for grim conversation."

"There's something I must tell you, Michael."

"Of course, but not here. You must be dead on your feet. Do you think anyone would shrivel with curiosity if I went to your room?"

I smiled. "I don't think so."

We went upstairs. Michael's arm stayed around me and I was grateful for the support. All at once the enormity of what I had to say overcame me. I hardly knew where to begin. When we were settled in armchair and chaise, though, I started the long, incredible story—a story which began in the dustiest reaches of the Bodleian Library and ended with a lead cross I'd held in my hands.

When I was finished, Michael sat quietly. I'd watched his face register curiosity, dismay at my trip through the tunnel, and finally a rare kind of wonderment.

"So fairy tales really *do* come true."

"It isn't a fairy tale, Michael."

"I know . . . I know . . . but it might as well be. The whole thing is simply unbelievable."

"See the cross and then you'll believe it."

"You left it there?"

"I photographed it, Michael, but I had to leave it. I don't know who put it there and what might happen if it was found missing. The Superintendent should deal with this."

"You're right, of course, Beth. I suppose you made the connection with Geoffrey?"

"With his murder, you mean? Yes. He put all the pieces together . . . as I did . . . and was killed so he wouldn't tell anyone."

"You realize that puts you in an unenviable position."

"But nobody *saw* me, Michael."

"You're sure?"

"Absolutely."

"All right then. What we need is a plan. Whitelaw's due back late this evening, so your report to him will have to wait until then." He looked at his watch. I'm going to find Sir Edmund now, and tell him about Bullock and Gamble."

"Will you mention the cross?"

"No. I want to hear Whitelaw's advice first. Right now I think it's better that no one else knows." He stood up and looked down at me. "Beth, you should see your face . . . it's all ridges and furrows. Don't frown and don't worry. We'll work it out. I'll see you down in the dining room."

I closed the door behind Michael and leaned against it, exhausted. Then I went into the bath, soaked in a cloud of scent, applied some makeup, and put on my dress. The primping helped; I felt human again. The clothes I took off smelled of damp and earth—dank, underground smells. It was so good to be clean, to walk to the window and look at the moon, to breathe the sweet air.

I wished the night ahead were over, however. I dreaded the hours to come and the showdown with Gamble. With Whitelaw away, Ian gone, and David steeped in his own concerns, Michael and I would be coping alone.

It was after seven when I started down the corridor. I'd almost reached the staircase when I heard voices from the family suite on the opposite side. There was some argument, a single strangled cry, murmurs, then hopeless weeping. As I stood there, Lily and David came out of a room.

They were facing each other, oblivious to me, and David appeared to be holding Lily upright. She looked wild—distraught—a fragmented creature. I had the eerie thought that a piece of her might snap off in David's hands.

"You *must* take me with you."

"Sh . . . I will, Lily. We'll leave in the morning."

"The morning's too *late,*" she wailed. "We've got to go now . . . tonight."

"Stop that! You're being hysterical."

"David, *please.* If you ever cared for me, *please.* Do this one thing."

I saw David stiffen. "I won't jump on command anymore, Lily . . . my life has to make sense. I've arranged to leave in the morning. If you want to come with me, you're welcome."

Lily's head went up. "Can we go early?"

David heaved a sigh.

"All right, we'll do that. Come." He led her back toward her room. "Wash your face and then we'll go down."

"You do promise me, David."

"Yes. *Yes.* I promise."

They went inside and the hall was empty again. I felt I'd viewed an interlude danced by two puppets: David still fastened to strings pulled by Lily—and Lily groveling to a terror she'd never named.

Even in the shadowed corridor, with tears streaming down her face and her movements disjointed, Lily's unearthly beauty prevailed. The golden hair, the luminous eyes, the frail figure in the gossamer dress—she was more than any man could resist. I hoped David meant what he'd said earlier, that once Lily was deposited in London he would go his own way. But he was as human, as vulnerable as the rest of us. If he succumbed again, who could blame him?

26

Dinner that evening was a dismal meal—a mandatory drill with all the players strained and anxious. When I walked into the dining room, the faces circling the oak table confirmed my apprehensions. Doom and gloom sat everywhere.

Benson seemed a bundle of tics, crumbling biscuits to dust in his consommé, and maintaining a patter that made no sense whatever. Marsden was utterly subdued, consuming his food as though it were a punishment, his mind a thousand miles away. For once even Gamble was quiet, after an opening gambit directed at Lily.

Lily gave no notice of Gamble—or anyone else. She sat like an autistic child. I saw David put his arm around her, place a fork in her hand, whisper, cajole, stroke her shoulder. She sat unmoving through it all, her eyes blank, the hand never raising the fork.

I thought Michael's presence would cut through the tension, but when he bounded in there wasn't even a ripple of interest. I knew better than to look stirred or expectant myself, so I offered him a bland, casual glance while my questions drummed in my head. I wondered how Sir Edmund had taken the news of Bullock here at Thorn Hill—of Bullock and Gamble together. Would he see the sinister implications—and if so—would Gamble be dumped?

Michael tucked into his food with unusual gusto—which could mean he was giving one of his masterful performances, was heartened by his talk with Sir Edmund—or simply that he was hungry. With no one to talk to and nowhere to look, I sat unhappily silent myself.

The clock ticked, crystal chimed against crystal, dishes were served. The staff, sensing the mood, made particular effort. Smiling, they bore in trays of lamb, sprout flowerlets, wheat gems, butter curls, glistening relishes, tilted salvers this way and that, whisked at the cloth, offered more wine—all to stony indifference. I felt for them, but remained dumb and still, as glum as the others.

We had progressed to sorbet, when Lily stood up. She clutched the edge of the table, wavering, but her voice was steady enough. "I'm going upstairs," she announced to no one in particular. David started to rise, but she stopped him. "I'll be all right. I'm going to bed."

It seemed her first sensible move. After a full night's rest she would feel better, look less ravaged, be fit for the trip back to London. I saw David watching her as she wove her way out, ready to spring up if she needed assistance. When Lily had left I assumed he'd relax a bit, but he alternated between toying irritably with his food and giving long, exasperated looks around the room. Trapped looks.

Everyone at Thorn Hill seemed trapped tonight—no one more so than Sir Edmund himself. I pictured him alone in his quarters upstairs, deep in a welter of business papers, and I thought: what would life at Thorn Hill be like now if Margaret Littell had lived?

She would be fortyish now, graying perhaps, but still with that brightness and fairness of skin which seems to last an Englishwoman's lifetime. I could see her presiding at this table tonight, all chitchat and country warmth, a senior player on the domestic scene, her girlish reticence matured into steady charm and graceful bonhomie.

She would never have tolerated this surly group. Good neighbors would be sitting here now—stolid, rosy folk with talk about school funds and church bazaars, about horses, dogs, and gardens. Every ordinary word would have been a comfort to Sir Edmund, who would not have come home to some empty room, but to the open arms of a loving woman. Just at that moment, Sir Edmund walked in.

His attitude was brisk. "John," he said to Benson, "I've left those papers on my desk with full instructions. If you read them through tonight, you can start processing them in London in the morning."

"I'll get them now," Benson said, and left.

Sir Edmund turned to Marsden. "Old Mr. Craddock has offered us his farm . . . he's going to Lewes to live with his sister. The lawyers will draw up the contracts, of course, but some personal attention would mean a lot to him. I'd like you to talk over the arrangements and ease the move in any way you can."

"I'll do that," Marsden said.

"He'd be home now. Why don't you go over there tonight?"

I saw that Marsden was surprised. There was a brief moment when his eyes widened and his mouth opened, as if he were about to protest. But he covered quickly, got up, said good-night, and walked out.

Sir Edmund focused next on David. "I understand you are leaving us in the next day or two, Mr. Cheney."

"Actually, I'm going back to London tomorrow."

"Tomorrow?"

"Yes." David looked uncomfortable. I knew what bothered him. He could hardly add ". . . and at her hysterical insistence, I'm taking your daughter with me." Instead he said, "I've been too long away from my play. Rehearsals are on and some revisions are needed."

"I see. That would be urgent. Well then, you'll have packing to do tonight?"

"I've just a few things. I can throw them together tomorrow," David said, his eyes veering from Sir Edmund to Michael to Gamble and back to Littell. I could see the playwright at work, sensing a private drama unfolding. The scene *did* have a theatrical quality—the flickering candles lighting, then shadowing, the faces around the table, the air heavy with unspoken questions. Was Sir Edmund preparing a confrontation between Michael and Gamble? Would Gamble have to answer for Bullock here and now?

"Of course." Sir Edmund paused. "And you, Mr. Grandville . . . you're still engrossed in your film, I suppose?"

"Now that the filming is finished, the next step is editing."

"And where is that done?"

"In London. I'll be going to London myself in the next day or two. Miss Kendall will go with me, of course."

"Will you do the editing yourself?"

"I'm afraid I'm not expert enough for that work, Sir Edmund. I've hired a cutter whom I hope to assist. In a way editing is the most creative part of moviemaking . . . the cutting, splicing, and putting together. It's a painstaking process."

"Takes a long while?"

"It takes concentration—a night-and-day job."

"When the editing's finished, what is the next step?"

"Then it's off to New York to screen the film for the network, arrange the scheduling, and work up the whole promotion effort . . . advertising, media coverage. All the essentials."

"That sounds like a lot of work."

"It is, but I'm looking forward to it."

"So you'd be anxious to get back to London yourself?"

"Naturally. Yes."

"Of course. Well, I wish you good luck."

Littell sat back and made a few more remarks—all time-killing and pointless. It had become such a strange conversation. I could see Michael hadn't caught the drift of it either; we stared at each other and then looked at Gamble. He was wearing a vapid smile and seemed to find nothing amiss. In the momentary silence I could hear the patter of soft rain against the leaded windowpanes behind me. And then another noise, far off. A siren?

"I want to thank you, Sir Edmund," Michael said.

"Pardon?"

"I want to thank you for your cooperation . . . for allowing us to film the dig."

"Ah, yes. Well, there is so much hard work involved . . . so many people. I thought it only fair to acknowledge their efforts."

"Frankly I think it will be wasted on an American audience," Gamble said.

"Wasted?" Michael asked.

"Just that. These remnants of the past mean so little to Americans . . . what interests them is a new car or some kind of cleaning machine. People sifting patches of earth will just look silly to them."

"This may astonish you, Gamble, but we have archeologists in America too. Accomplished ones."

"I'm not speaking of the few exceptions, I'm thinking of your masses. They couldn't care less about antiquity and tradition. It's not their fault, I suppose. The motivation to preserve the past is instilled by breeding, and yours is a nation of immigrants . . . any scum who could dredge up the boat fare. What can you expect from a nation of mongrels?" Gamble smiled engagingly as he said this, as if he were making some convivial social point.

Michael started to rise, but David's hand shot out, grabbing his forearm.

"That's what he wants, friend. Don't oblige him."

"Michael," I pleaded.

"Stop this," Sir Edmund said. "Stop it at once."

We froze then, in an awkward tableau—Gamble still smiling, Michael held firmly by David, me half out of my chair. The moment flew. Before anyone could catch their breath, we were all aware of doors slamming outside, a shuffle of footsteps, a medley of voices—some of them loud. There was a knock, and Benson came in.

Something's terribly wrong, I thought. Benson had the parchment face and flaccid jaw of someone in shock. Constable Mickle was at his elbow.

"Sir Edmund," Benson said, and Littell went out into the hall with them. There was subdued conversation, then Benson was back.

"There's been an accident," he said, looking down at the table. "It's Miss Felicia. She took a car and . . . and must have been going very fast. The car overturned on the curve just beyond the gates. Sir Edmund's going to her now. I think someone should go with him."

"Lily!" David cried hoarsely. He and Gamble rushed into the hall.

Michael followed. "I'm going too."

"Michael . . . "

"Stay here, Beth. It may be bad."

Benson had sunk into a chair. The room was utterly quiet now, so the sound of rain dashing against the windows was plain.

"Do you know?" I asked. "*Is* it bad, Mr. Benson?"

Benson looked at me. "I couldn't tell him. No one could tell him."

"Tell him? Tell him what?"

"Miss Felicia is dead."

27

The boy walked down Oxford's High Street, sidestepping the bicyclists and turning north at the covered market. He took no notice of the students or homebound shopkeepers, and stopped only once to look at his watch. Presently, he turned in at a sagging Victorian house, and checked his watch again. He'd been out fifteen minutes, precisely.

Upstairs, the flat was bare except for a cot, card table, and chair. He went directly to the flat's only cupboard, tested the knob, then crossed to the window. The street looked commonplace and respectable, drearily so. There was no Oxford grandeur in this little road. The boy thought of his own ancient school and the green fields around it. He'd loved it, but life held better things now. He pulled down the shade.

The key to the cupboard hung around his neck on a chain; its interior smelled like old sponges. He pulled at the string to the overhead light. Two boxes sat on the floor and, off to one side, a fawn tennis bag. The boy opened the first box—the cylinder lay in its Styrofoam bed. In the second box the other components were nested, protected. He lifted the canvas bag into the room, unzipped it, and pulled out the contents. They uncoiled like a snake.

The fitting had to be done very carefully, and reminded him of holidays, of pantomime costumes. He stepped into the bathroom to view the re-

sults. The mirror had been propped, cater-cornered, on the high molding—he twisted about to get the effect.

Two lenses stared out of the khaki base, and the snout of the mask sagged down obscenely. The eyepieces were so thick that his head seemed a shadow inside; when he turned, the snout bobbled. He went back to the cupboard, kneeling to put the mask in its box. As he rose, he heard the pealing of evening chimes and remembered why Oxford had never been bombed: Hitler had coveted it.

28

Dead.

Benson's eyes were brimming. Was he grieving for Lily or for her father, I wondered. Poor, tormented Lily. It was tragic to have that youth and beauty stilled, that lithe and silken body broken—flung in a ditch or trapped in a ratchet of steel. Horrible.

My own sorrow surprised me. I found it difficult to speak for a moment, then I put a hand on Benson's shoulder and asked, "Where was she going?"

He looked at me. "Going? She was headed toward London."

Of course. Lily had not waited for David. "I heard . . . I knew she wanted to go. I thought she planned to leave tomorrow with Mr. Cheney."

"She took Mr. Grandville's car."

"Michael's? But why . . ." Then I saw what had happened. Lily had pretended to go to bed, but had run to the garage instead. She'd simply searched every vehicle until she'd found one with keys. I'd seen Michael tuck his into the visor—it was, after all, not a public street but a private garage.

Benson put his head in his hands. "No one knows why she was leaving."

But I knew—knew something had frightened Lily badly

enough to send her careening down the wet and pitch-black London road. Frightened her to death. I patted Benson in one of those futile gestures one makes to succor the bereaved, and went upstairs to my room.

Its comfort seemed insidious. The marquetry tables and Minton figurines stood like props in a backdrop of normalcy—of luxury—but they did not reassure. The crewelwork draperies—layer upon woolen layer, fold after fold—could protect against wind and storm, but not the evil which seeped through every crevice in this house.

What was happening? First Geoffrey, now Lily—and up in London, Jock Magee. Events were moving too fast: Bullock and Gamble, the tunnel, the chamber, the cross. The cross. I sat on the bed and remembered its slate-gray surface, cold to the touch, and the primitive lettering. I'd thought Geoffrey had found jewelry—baubles—but what he'd discovered had made thoughts of treasure pall.

The cross was a certified icon, a chalice, a grail, the spirit of Arthur. In the right hands it could lift a sense of doom, resurrect glories, and bolster British spirits sky-high.

In the wrong hands it would serve as a weapon. It could be brandished—removed from the tunnel and used to further some lunatic movement. I could see it flaunted in London. "Follow Arthur," its captors would chant. "Follow us." And followers they would have—the deprived, the dissatisfied workers, the naïve, the stupid—the young. I shuddered. The young would join first—a new legion for Arthur.

Where had the cross come from? Who had been hiding it? Who had constructed that altar and put the cross on it? As I sat there, a sickening realization began and swelled to an anguished peak. *I should never have left it.* I'd wanted Whitelaw to see the cross in its place in that room, but suppose he came back to find nothing? Suppose the tunnel people, whoever they were, took it and went away? The cross might then disappear for hundreds of years, lost to England again. Or worse, it might emerge elsewhere, used as a banner to hail every twist of a new barbarity. The cross was the key and I'd left it behind.

Before my thoughts were fully resolved, before I let myself dwell on the pitfalls, before my own actions were clear to me—I was dressing. Sweater, warm socks, boots, raincoat, scarf. Torch in hand. I slipped down the stairs and out the front door, relieved to meet no one. I kept the headlights off while I eased out the Cortina and drove away from the house, switching them on only when the trees served as a shield.

My movements were as mysterious to me as they would have been to any onlooker. I was driven by instinct—hiding myself from the household, skulking out through the night. I had one idea: save the cross. Creep back through the tunnel, grab it, and run. Run to the car and drive away from Thorn Hill—not all the way to London perhaps, but to some inn where I could spend the night, safe with the cross. Tomorrow morning I would take it directly to the British Museum. Whoever wished to claim it *then* could do so through the proper channels.

I ran through the manor gates onto the road, and paused. Half a mile away the London route was blocked. The flashing lights of the police cars pierced the fog, and I could hear distorted voices on the car radios—constricted, bullhorn squawks. I turned the car to the right and drove through the village. There wasn't a soul about, so I judged news of the accident hadn't spread beyond the manor. Better for me; better to slip by unnoticed.

The lane was bumpy and the darkness so complete that the church and outbuildings loomed like three phantoms. I drove on a bit, around a further bend, and parked close to some bushes. I'd thought to camouflage the car, but I paid for my caution. The rain picked up midway back to the track, and when I finally unlatched the ancient door I was drenched and mud spattered.

I stepped inside and stood with my shoulder blades brushing the pitted old wood. The light from my torch danced in front of me, dipping and rising in my wavering hand. Cold. The outbuilding had been cold before, but not like this—the walls oozed a malignant dampness and chill. I made myself cross the room, lift the pincers, and pull the rear stone. It slid forward as easily as before and I cast my torch down the staircase. Down into that hole in the ground.

You did it before, I thought. Before you knew where the tunnel ended and what lay ahead. It's empty down there—just a passage, a room, and the cross. Ten minutes to get it, then out to the car and away. Cold won't hurt you. Darkness won't hurt you. What are you waiting for?

I climbed down, step by slippery step, scrabbling for handholds, then walked into the tunnel. Quickly. I must go quickly, not pausing, not thinking. If I stopped, I would panic.

The tunnel was dry, although there was a murmur off in the distance, which I thought was the echo of water dripping somewhere. I went as fast as I could, feeling the downward slope as the tunnel expanded, cautiously rounding each bend, and I came to the fork sooner than I expected. The linteled doorway sat just ahead and the rest of the passage continued. I shot my light into *that* blackness and shivered—someone could walk that way and never be seen or heard from again.

The doorway, at least, was familiar. I stepped through it and began casting my torch about, searching for the battery lantern. It should have been right at the entrance, but wasn't. I felt my first spasm of fear. I needed that light. I couldn't bear the thought of fumbling about without it. I began to move in circles, searching the floor, tapping the stones with my outstretched foot. Then I found it, ten feet away. It had clearly been moved: the tunnel people must have come back. I switched on the lantern, moved into the room—and gasped. The benches were gone and the high wooden table stood there alone. The square of green felt still covered its top.

Six steps—eight steps—twelve steps to the table. Praying now, I lifted the felt and, as before—found the cross. I felt my eyes filling with tears of relief. It was so simple, so plain—but no jeweled scepter, no imperial crown was more precious to England than this leaden object which had lain on King Arthur's breast.

I took the challis scarf from my head and wrapped the cross in it, then redraped the felt. The table must look untouched. At the room entrance I set down the lantern roughly where I'd picked it up and—torch in one hand, cross in the other—started into the passage.

And stopped. The murmur of dripping water was louder and now seemed to come from the other direction. But the tunnel had been dry all the way. Where could water be running? I must keep my head. Just a short run to the car, and an end to this. I'd drive away from Thorn Hill and never come back. Never. I'd meet Michael in London and there it would all seem like a dream. Not a dream—a nightmare. I stopped again. The murmur wasn't water at all. It was *conversation.*

People were talking in the tunnel ahead. The sound was too faint to pick up words—but it grew as I stood there. They were coming this way. They were blocking the route to the staircase. I was trapped.

Fright spurred me then. I groped my way back to the entrance and stood there, agonizing. The voices were louder now. Where could I hide? Not in the room. I'd explored it before and knew there was no alcove large enough. There was simply a table—a bare table now. The cross's custodians were seconds away and the cross was here in my hands.

I wrenched myself forward and—sobbing—ran into the passage extension. Ran into the void.

29

I'd run deep into the passage before the hysteria ebbed, before I slowed down to take stock. My breath was coming in wheezing gasps, and my heart pumping piston-fast in my chest, when I finally sagged against the tunnel wall, then slithered down to the floor. I must think. I must calm myself. I'd taken a desperate chance, plunging into the tunnel, not knowing what lay ahead. I still didn't know, and I'd have to move carefully.

Still breathing raggedly, I began gathering my options around me—few though they were. On the plus side I was sound and uninjured, and my torch worked. Straining into the darkness, I could hear no sounds of pursuit, so whoever was walking through the tunnel didn't know I was there.

On the debit side, my way out was blocked. The most favorable scenario had the tunnel people going into the chamber, attending to their business there, and leaving without realizing the cross was gone. That was possible, I thought, but unlikely. My best hope was that they would find the cross missing and go tearing back to the tunnel entrance. But that way was by no means a certainty: they might choose to search this way. I must find someplace to hide—and quick.

I got to my feet and moved forward cautiously, casting my light from side to side as I walked, searching the walls for some opening, some crevice into which I could press myself. The stones in this section were huge and irregular, but they all fit together in a smooth giant jigsaw. There was no opening at all.

What frightened me most was not knowing how far the passage extended. I was moving into a pit which could claim me forever. If I took a wrong turn I might lose myself in some ancient labyrinth. If I fell I might stay where I dropped, unable to crawl back to the light. And if the tunnel people caught up with me, what better spot for a burial place? Who knew what grisly rituals they performed in that chamber?

Desperate, I crept ahead, forcing myself to go slowly. I'd moved about fifty halting steps when my light picked up a gap in the wall ahead. It was a slit, barely two feet across, but wide enough for a single person to squeeze through. I did so, and found myself in a narrow, rockbound aperture with a sloping floor.

I kept fighting a rising, quavering panic. I was entombed. Trapped in a cave within a cave, on a path going nowhere. Even if I remained undiscovered, how would I find my way back? My knees turned to mush, and I tottered, throwing up the palms of my hands and scraping both on the rockface.

I steadied myself and the pain cleared my head. What choice did I have? There were people moving out there who were not bothered by scruples—Geoffrey had been killed with cold efficiency. My only chance was to find a niche a little further along, crouch there and wait. I looked at my watch—ten minutes past nine. I'd wait until ten. If I hadn't been discovered by then—dragged from my hiding place—I'd try to make it back to the stairs.

Twenty paces further I found a place I felt would be safe—far enough from prying lights, but not too deep in the pit. I pulled my coat tight around me and was about to sit down, when I became aware of the strangest smell—piercing and acrid. I turned and saw a flicker of something ahead. A light. My stomach turned then and I felt sick and defenseless. Was there another group waiting ahead of me?

I stood, scarcely breathing, and listened. No sound. Could the light mean an exit, another way out? I crept along, hugging the wall, measuring each step, dreading the errant, clattering pebble. The light ahead darted in the tunnel drafts. It must be a candle, but who would light a candle down here? "Damned if you do, and damned if you don't" the doggerel ran. It was true. If I didn't take this chance, I would surely be lost. The light *could* mean escape—another route out and a brief run to safety.

My greatest ally was the silence ahead. If there were people, I reasoned, there would have to be noise. Unless—my heart sank as I thought of it—unless there was a single person stationed there, guarding an exit; listening as I made my clumsy, and what seemed to me clamorous, way to his lair. But there was no guard. What I advanced to find was yet another room—this one so strange that I stopped on its threshold to stare in surprise.

It was piled high with boxes—wooden crates on which several oil lanterns sat. In their glimmer I could see that the crates had been numbered, and that there were avenues between them—as if workmen had moved back and forth, toting up shipments. The edge of one box had been pried partly open. I walked up to it, shone my torch inside, and recoiled. Guns. I could see the wooden stocks and steely barrels of dozens of guns. There must be thousands of guns in this room.

"What an odd place to find you, Miss Kendall," a voice said behind me.

30

I turned. Keith Gamble stood in the entry, backed by three students.

"Though I can't say I'm really surprised," he continued. "Watching you, I couldn't tell whether it was a definite mission or simple stupidity that drove you to snoop so much. You've been lamentably obvious." He smiled. "No matter, the result is the same. You're going to be squelched now, Miss Kendall. Stoppered."

Instinctively, I stepped back—into the rough edge of a crate. "I . . . I've lost my way."

"I think that's safe to say. I hope you're not going to try one of those innocence routines. It would be pointless."

He was right. The students had moved forward menacingly. I recognized one of them. He was as fair as Gamble, but bigger, and he kept opening and closing his fists. His hands were huge. Big enough, I thought numbly, to break me in two. It would be futile to lie now.

"What is this place?" I countered. "What does it mean?"

"It's an arsenal, Miss Kendall. One of many. And what it *means* is a better England . . . militarily and economically strong. It means a New Age. We have platoons of young men, all as fine as these, stationed around the country. We've ammunition now . . . arms which took us a long time to collect. We have a plan. *And,"* he wrenched the cross from my hand and tore the scarf away, "we have an emblem too."

He regarded the cross with amusement. "I'm told it's genuine but that's hardly crucial . . . any piece of old metal or old bag of bones would do. What's important is that it's *believed* to be genuine. The cross will serve us well. It validates our function."

"And gives you license to kill?"

"Meaning Trehane, I suppose. Geoffrey got wind of us, and his timing was bad. Another few weeks and it wouldn't have mattered. But our Philip saw to him, didn't you, Phil?"

The big student nodded.

Geoffrey. I could only think of how gentle he'd been. "Murderer."

Gamble stepped up so quickly that I scarcely noticed the movement—or the arm that swung in a wide arc toward me. The blow cracked in my head—more shock than pain at first—then everything faded. I staggered and fell to my knees.

"That should put you in touch with reality," Gamble said.

The room righted itself by degrees. First I saw the splintery side of a box, then noticed my own hands on the floor. They were supporting me. I was crouched like an animal. There was a semicircle of boots and heavy shoes set around. I'd begun laboriously counting them—two, four—when one of the pair advanced and a hand hooked under my armpit, pulling me upright. That hurt, and I turned to protest. It was the student, Philip, who held me.

Gamble laughed when I flinched away. "I know these lessons are hard, Miss Kendall, but they're necessary. We'll have to detain you awhile . . . we may need you as bait."

"Michael . . . "

"You can forget about him. Grandville shouldn't have been

so rash, threatening to tell Whitelaw about Bullock. That stupid old sod . . . I could have strangled him for coming here.

"Your Michael got worrisome, so we fixed his car. If he didn't use it tonight, there would have been other ways. He could have been waylaid and coshed, dropped in a pond somewhere." His face clouded. "Lily took the car instead. Poor, silly girl. I told her I'd care for her, that there was no need to panic. She wouldn't listen to me. She'd listen to all those other degenerates, but never to me."

I stared at him, aghast.

"Lily could never grasp the New Age. She said it frightened her. *Frightened her,* mind you. I told her that after the transition she would live like a princess, but she never believed me.

"It won't be one of those spartan dominions. We're keeping the pageantry. We'd like to keep the monarchy too, if we can show the Royal Family that the people will suffer without them. The cross will be worshipped as the crux of our heritage. We want to glorify England, you see, not diminish her. The people will like that . . . they love all the splendor."

I found my voice then. "You're mad. Can't you see you'll never be allowed to do what you plan? Never."

"Indeed. Who will stop us?"

"The army . . . the police . . . "

"But many police and military men are supporting us. What you don't understand, Miss Kendall . . . what so many don't understand . . . is that the people are yearning for change. Yearning for leadership, for a purified Britain. They know they'll get no help from democracy. Democracy, which started so bravely, is a toothless dog waiting to die. Communism is abhorrent to Britons. So what is left?" He moved closer. "We are.

"Britain's strength is young men like these," he waved toward the students, "men who are dedicated in a way that neither you nor your soft Grandville could know. Look at them." He grasped my chin in an iron grip and dragged me toward one of the boys. "This is the Englishman of the future . . . well schooled, well trained, and committed."

The boy's eyes were hooded and blank. Where had I seen that look before? Then I remembered. In a narrow Boston street a young man had walked up to me, preaching the cult of some swami. He was hawking a pitiful journal, spewing the text as if his mouth were a spigot. Brainwashed. The eyes bleached of expression. If Gamble had armies of mutants like these, who could stop him, indeed?

"When we begin getting results," Gamble continued, "when the people see their lives are better in every way, we'll have all the support we need. But that shouldn't concern you." He gathered the front of my coat in both hands and pulled me toward him. "When *that* happy day arrives, you'll be long since gone."

His face twisted with rage and grief. "If it weren't for you and Grandville and your infernal meddling, Lily would be alive now. Alive! If you'd kept to yourselves, we wouldn't have had to alter the car. That's *your* fault, yours and his . . . and I'll never forget it.

"Do you know how she died? When the car overturned, the gas tank exploded. She was burned to a crisp. There wasn't enough of her left to put in a handkerchief."

He pulled the coat tighter. "When it's your turn to go, I'll remember. There'll be a treat ready for you and your friend. And when we're finished, you'll be fed to some bog. There won't be a trace left of either of you."

I stood frozen in horror.

Never loosening his grip, Gamble shouted and several more students appeared. They picked up some lists and resumed their inventory with countinghouse diligence, while Gamble called out instructions. That finished, he threw me at Philip.

"Take her up to the gallery . . . no one goes there. We'll catch up with Grandville." He smiled. "Miss Kendall has such a fondness for antiquities . . . it should please her to spend her last hours in the oldest part of the house."

I was pinioned and tied at once. My own scarf was used as a gag. I was handled so roughly and it all happened so swiftly that a queer kind of dizziness struck.

I'm going to fall again, I thought, and I can't help myself. My face is going to hit the stone floor.

But before that could happen, something coarse and voluminous was thrown over my head. I sank into blackness.

31

I awoke in a vast space, raising my head to blink at the dark corners of a peculiar arena. There was a wall behind my back; I could sense it. But the areas to my left and right stretched out into chilling infinity. Then I understood. I was in the gallery at the top of the house.

I ached. I was bound to some tall chair, my ankles lashed to its legs, the rest tied to its upright back. Every part of me seemed to hurt, but particularly my head and neck. They must have fallen forward while I was unconscious, drooping puppet-like onto my chest.

I'd seen the gallery before in the daytime, with the sunlight streaming through its oriel windows. It ran the whole width of the house, almost two hundred feet, a graceful expanse of oak paneling, polished floor, and whorled Flemish patterns in the plasterwork ceiling.

At night its vastness was menacing. The faintest shimmer of moonlight crept in, but I had to peer in all directions—blinking and straining against my bonds—to confirm I was completely alone. Alone with the chairs, the portraits, and whatever ghosts still used this room for their promenades.

It was terribly cold. For some reason my coat had been

stripped off and the rest of my clothes were still damp from the rain. I sat sodden and miserable, skewered by thoughts of what was to come.

I was going to die.

I'd spent my twenties airily acknowledging death. "We are all mortal," I'd said to my girls and they had regarded me blandly. I thought I wanted to plant thoughts of the past, give inklings of the passage of time. I knew *now* that I'd wanted to lump us together. We weren't so far removed, were we—the girls with the shining hair, the perfect skin, the long, strong limbs—and myself? Death was something that surely came when one was ready to go—gnarled and implacable in the face of its rigors.

Death was going to happen to me—and soon—but that wasn't the worst of it. The worst part was my fear for Michael. He was running about out there—unawares—unprepared for those who were primed to attack him, and there was no way I could warn him.

I remembered a particular day we had shared; the one I thought the most perfect in that long string of days. Michael had hired a seaplane and we'd gone up to the Vineyard for lunch. Simply that. We'd boarded the tiny craft in the East River and were in Edgartown in an hour. After lunch, a boat brought us to where the plane bobbed in the sea, and we took off for Manhattan. We'd approached the city in the late afternoon. It sat between the two rivers like a huge confection, its spires twirled and elegant in the setting sun. At that moment I'd looked across the little cabin at Michael and felt a surge of the keenest—the most childlike—pleasure and joy.

There had not been another such perfect day. Michael had departed and the lost years intervened. Now we would have no time together at all—there were no days, nights, or weeks to look forward to. I let my head sag down on my chest again and—despairingly—started to cry.

I must have sat there for hours. My limbs lost all feeling, my wrists were an agony. Sometimes I would start at the sound of my own muffled voice, calling in terror. I was—for the hundredth time—struggling against the ropes, hoping to ease them, when I heard a noise at the end of the gallery. Stiff-necked, I painfully craned around, straining to see in the dark. Nothing. The room seemed as silent and dim as before. Then the noise was repeated, and a sliver of light appeared in the corner. The door was opening—did open—the light entered and the door closed again. Someone was standing here in the room with me.

The light paused, hung in space. A greater dread than I'd ever known enveloped me and I stared down that endless room, transfixed. The light began to advance. Someone called my name—the light moved more quickly—and Sir Edmund came up to me.

The shock of relief was so great that I sagged back again, feeling faint. Sir Edmund seemed profoundly distressed. He pulled a small table around, set his lamp on it, and loosened my gag.

"Miss Kendall, are you all right?"

It was a moment before I could speak. "I . . . I think so. It's cold though. I'm cold." My mouth felt sore. "Sir Edmund, I'm so glad you're here. How did you . . . "

"Just a minute." He moved into the shadows. I heard a tap on glass, an odd rattle, and then he was back. Incredibly, he was holding a small sword, which he drew out of its sheath.

"From the cabinet," he said. "Now you must stay absolutely still." Kneeling, he cut through the ropes at my ankles, then pulled the chair into the light and severed those at my shoulders and wrists. He took both of my hands in his and began rubbing them vigorously. "We must get the circulation going again. Can you move your feet?"

I tried, but the pain was intense.

"Flex them a little, if you can."

Michael. I must get to Michael. I tried to stand, but fell back.

Sir Edmund put his hand on my shoulder. "You mustn't think of walking just yet. The weakness will pass in a few minutes, but you must rest for a while."

He drew a chair away from the wall and sat down next to me. His face was drawn and his gestures mechanical. His eyes seemed to look past me, searching for someone else.

"You've heard what has happened to my poor little girl?" he asked, but didn't wait for my answer. "I keep thinking of her as she used to be, when she was small. She was such an innocent spirit then. No matter what she did later, I had to believe that that innocent spirit prevailed." He leaned toward me. "Can you understand that, Miss Kendall?"

"Sir Edmund, I'm so terribly sorry."

"I believe you are. You're a good person, I think. I'm sorry for *you.*"

"For me?"

"Sorry you've had this experience."

He went on. "I know Felicia's life would have been different if her mother had lived. My Margaret was so gentle, so patient . . . she would have been such a good influence. You'd have liked Margaret. She had your appreciation of what was enduring. We . . . Margaret and I . . . lived through a difficult period. We both knew the war had changed England, that the country we loved wasn't the same.

"We believed in the principle of aristocracy, you see . . . it's the aristocracy who've defended what's best in us. The English people used to support this natural order. They seemed to understand that certain of us led by divine right. But since the war their attitudes have been poisoned, and now the upper classes are besieged. If the upper classes are destroyed, I believe Britain is doomed. That can't be permitted. We must set it all straight again. You can see that, can't you?"

"I . . . I don't know."

"Please. Say you do see that."

"I see that."

"That's good. Margaret and I used to walk together and talk and talk. I know we shared something rare . . . she understood me perfectly. We talked about what was happening to England. She was expecting then, and we both swore we would protect what we could for our child.

"But then Margaret died." He paused. "Margaret died, and I found I couldn't raise our child alone. Not successfully. Not in a way which would keep her peaceful and happy, content with life at Thorn Hill. The culture snatched her away . . . a culture which fills our young people with degrading thoughts and gives them permission to lead degrading lives. I tried, but I failed, and Lily was lost."

He moved closer. "You've heard of the grail-keepers?"

"Grail-keepers?"

"A breed of men responsible for preserving the legends. The Littell family's grail was the cross. I was raised with it. It was sold to my grandfather years ago and has been at Thorn Hill ever since.

"It was known only to my grandfather, my father, and me. I was a sick child and had to stay home; my father would bring it to me in my room. Father let me hold the cross and he explained what it meant to us and to England. Father believed that when the moment was right, King Arthur would come forward and save England again. Not reincarnated, of course, but through the cross. He told me that if the moment didn't come in his lifetime, it might come in mine . . . and it has."

His face dulled as his mind skimmed the years. "Afterwards Geoffrey would give me my lessons, and then we'd march armies over the bed. Lead soldiers. Geoffrey would salute me. 'Mark, the most powerful Knight Commander,' he'd say . . . I was called

Mark as a child . . . and all the time I knew that I really *was* powerful, because of the cross."

He reached forward and grasped my arms. "I know you have seen the cross, so you understand what I'm saying. You can appreciate what my life has been like, knowing I'm heir to it. I think I'm privileged to *be* heir by a force which transcends the human experience. That force is Arthur's spirit returning. Will you believe that?"

His face was barely six inches away and his eyes searched mine anxiously. I tried to look calm—to *stay* calm—while a stream of the most harrowing thoughts raced through my head.

The cross belonged to Sir Edmund. It was his heritage as much as the manor house, Thorn Hill, and his fortune. The sick little boy had become a powerful man, moving in Europe's exalted spheres. But the corporate titan and the shrewd financier was still—at his core—a febrile child propped up in bed, fed legends of conquests, and consumed by a destiny mapped in the mists of England's beginnings. He thought of himself as Arthur's successor. In Arthur's name he would send legions of hollow-eyed boys, armed to the teeth, into English cities and towns.

There would be riots first, carefully staged—and sabotage, blamed on the immigrants. Every primitive fear would be stirred, then whipped to a pitch. There would be shooting, a surging mass in the streets, barricades overturned, murder, and anarchy rampant. I had a vision of men with clubs—pummelling, bludgeoning.

No—not just clubs. Instead I saw men in boiled leather jerkins, wielding iron-spiked spears, as the Dark Age returned.

I must get out of this room.

As if he'd read my mind, Sir Edmund's grip tightened. "It's a relief to tell this to you. This has all been a burden to me." Then he added quite reasonably, "but I must do this work because I was born to it, because Father and Grandfather told me to do it."

He's mad, I thought then.

He sat holding my arms, staring, and rocking a bit in the flickering lamplight. His shadow moved back and forth on the ceiling above us, darkening the whorled strapwork which patterned the plaster, circled arabesques running the gallery's length. Whirled patterns. Scrolls and spirals. Twisting. Intertwined. They looked eerily familiar, as though they'd coiled through my mind in a dream.

Geoffrey's doodle. It had worked the same scrolls and knots into a similar maze. The same patterns interwoven, repeated. The shadow moved again. Mark the baeddle, Geoffrey's paper had said. Baeddle was monster.

But Mark hadn't meant "watch" or "observe." Mark had meant—Mark—a little boy playing with soldiers, steeped in feverish visions, grappling with phantoms a thousand years old. The shadow moved on the ceiling. A tremor of horror shot through me. Mark the baeddle. *Mark the monster.*

Geoffrey had known.

32

Edmund Littell leaned forward again, his eyes fixed on my face. "Is this all clear to you now?"

"Clear?" Say anything. Fight for time. "Yes, Sir Edmund, I do understand."

"I'm so glad." He seemed immensely relieved. "I don't want you to think . . . " He hesitated. "I want you to know you have my respect. You are one of the few young people I've met with worthwhile ideals. But the circumstances . . . the position we find ourselves in . . . makes one course of action inevitable. And *that's* what I wanted to clarify . . . that there's no personal rancor involved."

He knows I'm to be killed.

"It's not just you," he continued. "We'll all have to sacrifice . . . but think of what good can be done. We can build a new spirit of patriotism. We can vanquish the modern view, which does so little to nourish the soul. And," his voice grew thick with disgust, "we can do away with vermin like Jock Magee.

"Magee had to pay for what he did to my Lily. She thought he was wonderful. Wonderful . . . that subanimal creature. He debased her as he debased other young women, then moved along with his pack. They flock together . . . these venal young men . . . polluting the earth, ruining innocent children. Well, Jock Magee won't corrupt anyone else and maybe his death will enlighten the others."

"Sir Edmund . . . "

"Sh——" He put up his hand. "You mustn't be frightened. Death can be many things. With Magee, death served as a lesson. For others . . . such as yourself . . . it can be a deep, peaceful sleep. In the war many died. I saw many deaths myself. Good men . . . good friends . . . they died for a purpose. And so will you. This is a kind of war. Your death will be meaningful."

Run. I must run to the end of the gallery. The door might be locked, but I must try to get out. Try to live.

Sir Edmund was sitting so close. His hands held mine, our shoulders touched, and his gaze was unswerving and terrible—as if he could root out my thoughts. I edged away in what I hoped seemed a natural movement, and grimaced.

"Are you in pain?" His voice was remote, monotone.

"My ankle still hurts," I bent down, sliding my hands from his grasp, and made a pretense at massage. My shoes lay to one side—I'd be swifter without them. I knew he was watching; the move had achieved a barely perceptible distance between us. "Please give me a moment."

I could not see his face, but his body relaxed. It had to be *now.* Twisting away in one violent turn, I jumped to my feet and streaked into the black part of the room. I heard his grunt of surprise and saw the light dart as he shifted against it. Then he was on his feet too—and running—with a swiftness and ease that horrified me.

We were both running in darkness, but he knew every inch of the room. My mind sprinted ahead at a frenzied pace, trying to remember the door. Knob, latch, or pull? One lock or two? The wrong move, an instant's fumble, and I would be caught.

I was sobbing now, for lack of breath, and appalled by the rhythm of the feet pounding behind me. Too late, I remembered how fit Sir Edmund had been—his stocky form graceful in movement. He was gaining—the footfalls were closer.

I was aware of the frantic pad of my own stockinged feet, of the shadows that loomed from the faint glow behind us. My eyes bore into the dimness ahead, scanning its depths for the gallery's end. To the left. The light had entered to the left. The door must be there. He pulled nearer. I could hear his breathing—not panting like mine, but heavy and steady—an arm's length away. He had only to reach with both hands. I cried out in anguish.

Then he tripped, or slipped. I heard the shout and the thud as he crashed to the floor. The noise gave me impetus. I spurted ahead, mouthing gibberish prods to keep myself going.

I did not so much reach the door as slam into its thick oaken breadth with the full force of my body. My hands scrabbled dementedly over its surface—clawing at massive hinges, fumbling with the iron hardware below. A knob. There was an enormous knob, and a lock and a key. The key turned. I heard the lock respond. I grasped the knob, twisted it, pulled at the door.

At first I could not get it to move. Weeping, praying aloud, I tried again, pulling with all my strength. Slowly, ponderously, the door creaked toward me and opened—an inch, a sliver, a crack. There were lights; I could see the staircase below. If I could get down those first steps and turn at the landing . . .

Sir Edmund's hand clamped on my shoulder. "I'm sorry, Miss Kendall," he said almost sadly, "I can't let you go."

I screamed then, screamed into the narrowing crack as the door closed again—and I ducked deep beneath his arm, driving my elbow into his stomach. He snatched at me—part of my blouse came away—but I wriggled free, and bolted again.

Back. Racing back toward the light. Flying toward what? A dead end. The door would be locked now, and I was sure he'd pocketed the key. I was alone, with no one to help me and no other way out—fixed on this treadmill of horror.

The chair, lamp, and table ahead looked like a theatrical set for a tête-à-tête. A travesty. The glass cabinet doors shone in the lamplight.

The cabinet. Sir Edmund had gone to the cabinet and come back with the sword. I could see it now where he'd left it, leaning against the far chair. I ran to it, picked it up, and wheeled about to face my enemy.

He was quite far behind, and he was walking. Marching, really, at a clipped, parade-ground pace. Why should he run, I thought. He had his prey trapped. My hands shook so hard that I could barely hold the sword up.

He came nearer. "Miss Kendall, this is grotesque," he said icily. "Must I take that away from you?"

"Don't come near me, Sir Edmund. Stay back!"

"This is ridiculous. Gamble will be here any minute. Do you think you can hold us both off?"

I leaned on the chair for support. "Please, Sir Edmund. I don't want to hurt you."

"Hurt me?" He smiled at this foolish suggestion. "You'll never hurt me, Miss Kendall. You don't have it in you."

He made perfect sense. We weren't discussing a scratch or a wound. In order to keep him away, I'd have to impale him. I could never do that.

I wavered.

"Put the sword down," he commanded.

I lowered it.

"That's right. Just set it down on the floor."

I was so tired. What did it matter? Obediently, I let the sword drop.

"That's fine," he said. "Now we can . . . "

There was some sort of noise on the stairwell. Something was hitting the door. I heard shouts, but they were too faint, too far away. It could not be Gamble: he'd never make all that commotion. Sir Edmund turned, puzzled.

The pounding continued. Sir Edmund listened for scant minutes more, then he looked back at me. His face was flushed, his eyes wild. He reached forward and grabbed my wrist, wrenching so that I screamed again, dragging me around so I stood in front of him.

There were more shouts, a silence, a succession of gunshots. The door was hammered again; it gave way. At the dark end of the room, I saw several people come in—they rushed toward us.

I stiffened. Edmund Littell threw his left arm around my neck, choking me, pulling me close. I could feel his breath and the heave of his chest. His jaw bore into the side of my head. It moved—he was muttering. My own vision narrowed, began to fade.

And then Michael and Superintendent Whitelaw ran into the light.

Michael looked terrible, grim and distraught. He would have run up to us, but the Superintendent restrained him.

"Wait."

"He has Elizabeth . . . "

"I'm telling you, *wait.*" Whitelaw turned to the four men behind him—Constable Mickle, McGowan, the sergeant who'd been at Geoffrey's cottage and—perplexingly—Marsden. There were a few whispers and Mickle retreated.

Whitelaw stepped forward. "Sir Edmund, I am asking you to release Miss Kendall at once."

Littell did not speak.

"You must realize your position is hopeless. I've sent for more men."

"Lily . . . "

"What?"

Littell shifted me to one side. "I'd like to see my child before she's . . . I'd like to spend a few minutes with her."

"Sir Edmund," deep pity marked Whitelaw's face. "I wouldn't advise that."

"You wouldn't?" I felt Sir Edmund sag. "I see. Strange there was so much life in her and then . . . at the end . . . nothing left."

He stood silent. We all stood silent, cast into stone by the specter of death.

"Won't you come with us now?" Whitelaw asked.

Littell stirred. "Come where, Superintendent? To what haven?"

No one answered.

Littell sighed. Then he mumbled into my ear, "Bend down." We dipped quickly, in a parody of some gym exercise, and when we rose again Sir Edmund was holding the sword.

Michael cursed and moved closer.

"Stay back!" Whitelaw ordered, hanging onto his jacket.

"Miss Kendall isn't my enemy. I'd rather not hurt her," Littell said, "so I'm going to bargain with you."

"Bargain?"

"I'm going to trade her for a clear walk to that window," he waved toward the oriel bay.

"Sir Edmund . . . "

Littell raised the sword. "Don't cross me, Superintendent. I'm not asking for much."

"Very well . . . "

"Superintendent!"

"Be quiet, Grandville. All right, Sir Edmund, you have my word."

We walked backwards together, in a tense shuffling step; my head arced in the crook of his arm. It took an eternity to get to the window. The gallery stretched out ahead, forms dotting its gloom, but I could see only Michael. His eyes seemed to implore me, to send me some message.

We stopped in the curve of the bay. Sir Edmund let go of me, dropped the sword to the floor. I heard iron groan as the window was opened.

Then he turned me around. The wind was high; I could see the trees bending outside, dark shapes in the night. His face was composed. He looked at me in the same piercing way as the first night we met. And he murmured: " . . . I know not what I am,/Nor whence I am nor whether I be King./Behold, I seem but King among the dead."

He whirled me around again, and sent me spinning toward Michael. I felt Michael's arms folding around me. Then I mercifully fainted—but not before hearing the thud on the stone terrace below.

33

I was back in my room. I first saw the patterned canopy looming above, then Sally's face in a strange kind of blur, and then Michael.

He sat on the edge of the bed looking down at me, and he seemed so exhausted, so worn, that I instinctively reached out to touch him. He bent over and his lips brushed my cheek.

"Elizabeth. Dearest . . . "

"Michael . . . the gallery. Where . . . ?"

"I carried you down."

"I remember. I fainted."

"It was more than a faint. Shock, the doctor said. You've been out for two hours."

"Here you are, miss." Sally came into focus again. "Drink this. It's just juice. The doctor prescribed it."

Michael lifted me up while Sally plumped both my pillows. I was sipping the juice when those last, ghastly minutes came back.

"Michael! Sir Edmund . . . "

His face darkened. "He's dead, Elizabeth. He went out the window."

"I remember now. I heard it, Michael. The sound . . . "

"Sh—— darling. It's all over now. You're all right."

"Sir Edmund. Oh Michael, he was so pitiful."

"Pitiful and lethal," Michael said bitterly. "He almost killed you."

There was a knock at the door. Sally answered it, and then slipped out as the Superintendent walked in. He came over to the bed immediately, gave Michael a sober glance, shook his head quickly, then smiled at me.

"I'm glad to see those bright eyes open, Miss Kendall."

"Thank you. I seem to be all in one piece, Superintendent. What's happened?"

"Happened?"

"I saw you nod to Michael just now. Please tell me. I need to know."

Whitelaw pulled over a chair and sat down. "You're right, Miss Kendall. You do need to know. You deserve to know, after all you've been through. First, Sir Edmund is dead."

"Michael just told me."

"I see. Second, then . . . most of the students here have been rounded up and the arms and ammunition collected."

"Most of the students?" Michael asked.

"We're missing three. We think two are hiding on an abandoned farm at the edge of the village. We've surrounded the place. The other boy we can't find at all."

I put my glass down and sat up. "This other boy, Superintendent. Do you know his name?"

"Yes, we do. After some prodding, we got one of the others to tell us. His name is Atherton, Philip Atherton."

"Superintendent," I said unsteadily, "that's the boy who killed Geoffrey."

"We know that. Gamble told us. Mr. Gamble," his tone was laced with revulsion, "is in the full flush of confession. He's being taken to London now, but Philip Atherton's gone."

I had a sudden presentiment. A sense of foreboding grew as Michael and Whitelaw looked at me gloomily.

"And the cross. Michael . . . the cross," I heard myself whisper.

"The cross is gone too," Whitelaw said.

I realized afterwards that Sally must have come in again and made up a fire. As we talked, its warmth and aroma spread and its crack punctuated the Superintendent's narration. Painstakingly, patiently, he led Michael and me through the sickness that Gamble had called his New Age.

Edmund Littell had come to know Sidney Bullock fifteen years ago, when Bullock's image was still respectable and he could lend a sympathetic ear to Sir Edmund's fears for his nation. They seemed to share political views, and met periodically. In the winter of 1973–74, when the world oil crisis and the miners' strike had pushed Britain to the brink, Bullock had come to Sir Edmund and asked for support. He said he represented a group of men, corporate leaders, newspaper publishers, and retired army officers, who hoped to effect a coup. They wanted to form a new government, Bullock asserted—a strong government which could resist the impending chaos and shift Britain back from the welfare state to what she'd once been.

Bullock found a willing listener—he'd caught Sir Edmund at a vulnerable time. Littell had been brooding about what he considered the decay of his country. He fiercely believed England should be ruled by the upper classes—"persons of breeding"—and that upsetting those historic patterns was a fatal mistake. He was aghast at what he saw going on all around him—modern Britain seemed to represent the erosion of every value he cherished.

I asked, "Was he unbalanced then?"

"On the way," Whitelaw replied. "What was making him desperate was Lily's behavior. She had already left school and was making the rounds of London's seamier billets. She'd toyed with a lot of men before she reached Jock."

"So I heard."

"Sir Edmund began to rail at a society which failed its children so dismally . . . building brutes into heroes. He has company there . . . many parents feel we've been skirting Gomorrah.

"Littell had pledged his support to Bullock," Whitelaw continued, "but then made a private decision. Since he had no more faith in the group Bullock represented than the existing government, he would take matters into his own hands. That day marked a turning point in the Bullock-Littell relationship. Bullock thought Sir Edmund a political innocent who could be used for his money and influence. Littell was determined to use Bullock for his *own* ends. In such a power play, Bullock hadn't a chance. He planted Keith Gamble . . . a hanger-on of the lunatic fringe . . . so he could keep Sir Edmund under control. But Gamble became Sir Edmund's man . . . greener grass at Thorn Hill."

Littell had guessed, rightly, that the crisis would pass and the urge toward revolution evaporate. But there were thousands of Britons—civil servants, police officers, military men, and ordinary citizens—who would remain disaffected. He believed Bullock could deliver this group when they were needed—that his army and Bullock's would join.

"As time passed, though," Whitelaw added, "Bullock felt Littell's plans were becoming maniacal. In point of fact, they were."

"When you were taking Gamble out to the car, I heard him shouting about gas and cylinders," Michael said.

Whitelaw looked grim. "I hope no one else heard . . . we don't want a general panic. I'll have to prevail upon Gamble to keep his mouth shut." He looked gravely at both of us. "I'm breaking the rules, but I see no alternative. Facts are better than surmise, and you have so much to keep to yourselves anyway . . ."

Sir Edmund had structured a plan for a government which he called the New Age and Keith Gamble began recruiting young men—both undergraduates and working-class boys—for his troops. The prime candidates were rotated at Thorn Hill, but there were bases all over the country. The process took several years. While the recruits were being trained, guns and ammunition were being amassed—either stolen domestically or smuggled from abroad.

"We began getting peculiar reports from remote sites—tiny towns. The dig at Thorn Hill was a natural cover, but it was hard to invent plausible reasons for the other bases. We looked at some and they seemed to be what they said they were . . . gun clubs, sports clubs, camps . . . one appropriately called a psychiatric center. The groups were concentrated in Yorkshire and the Border country. Tom Marsden began hearing rumors from his home district."

"Marsden," I said. "He came into the gallery with you . . . "

"One of our best men," Whitelaw said, "and a natural actor. Tom comes from those dales and he was troubled by what he was hearing. By the time he reported to us, though, we had another informant. One of the students. One who was not wholly brainwashed and managed to get away. We learned the main base was Thorn Hill and that Gamble was in charge of it. Marsden was able to latch onto a job as estate manager, but at this point we didn't fully realize what we were dealing with."

"And then *we* turned up," Michael added, "throwing a wrench in the machinery."

"You did that," Whitelaw agreed, "but you also served as a catalyst." He glanced at me. "Both of you."

"You know, Superintendent," Michael said slowly, "I never could understand why they let us come in the first place."

"I asked Gamble that myself," Whitelaw said. "It appears they were afraid of your influence."

"My *what?*"

"Influence. You may not take your position seriously, Grandville, but they surely did. To them you were a star with an international reputation. Sir Edmund felt you must have many London contacts and that these contacts would think it peculiar if he refused you permission to film. He feared they would think he was being unusually secretive about the dig and that he was really harboring a mammoth find. That would have brought *more* attention. So the idea was to allow your crew to come quickly, film, and get out. They felt an uprising would be a fait accompli before the film was processed."

"And would it have been?" Michael asked.

A look crossed the Superintendent's face which I found unnerving. A haunted, stricken look.

"Absolutely," he said. "They were ready to go. When you told me about the men in the garden, Miss Kendall, I realized they were moving arms. All the guns weren't in the tunnel cache . . . there were crates hidden at the student lodge and in a locked subbasement here at the house. And this was just one depot, of course. The stores here were duplicated in dozens of places."

Geoffrey Trehane, the Superintendent explained, had followed the Bodleian clues—as I later did—and had found the tunnel and cross. But Geoffrey had explored further and found the arms cache right away. One of the students reported to Gamble that Trehane had been seen near the outbuilding. Gamble had tapped the manor telephone to monitor Michael's calls and verify our backgrounds: our rooms had been searched for the same reason. Geoffrey's call to me was overheard, Gamble put two and two together, and realized that Geoffrey had to be stopped before he told anyone.

"I think Dr. Trehane realized the significance of the cross in the chamber," Whitelaw said somberly, "and furthermore understood that his old friend, Sir Edmund, was deeply involved."

"I'm sure of that, Superintendent," I said, describing the doodle.

"Trehane went to the church that morning to pray for guidance . . . and was killed there by Philip Atherton. Gamble is saying the death was an accident, but we will prove otherwise. My guess is that . . . knowing how close the men were . . . he told the same tale to Sir Edmund."

"Would Littell have believed that?" Michael asked.

"I think not. I think Trehane's death was a terrible shock and that he held himself responsible for it. But he couldn't bring Trehane back, and the movement was paramount. There was so much at stake that he did nothing. His grief and guilt began to overwhelm him . . . although his sanity was already being corroded by a decision he made many months ago. I'm coming to that."

Gamble and Atherton had left Geoffrey's body in the church, the Superintendent added, hoping it would look as though he'd been killed by a vagrant. They had taken his house keys out of his pocket and Gamble sent Atherton to search Geoffrey's house and eliminate any clues to the tunnel. Atherton had started to search, but never got to the papers because Mrs. Tierney had arrived at the kitchen door. Atherton dropped the keys on the peg, and ran.

"That was a blunder," Whitelaw added, "because they had locked the church behind them. Dr. Trehane's death gave me a reason for being at Thorn Hill, Miss Kendall. A sad reason, but one we utilized to the fullest. It's highly irregular to conduct an investigation from a private home, but we knew it would be a tremendous advantage to be here at the manor. When we made our request, there was no way Littell could refuse. So some of us were involved in investigating the murder, but many more in keeping the manor and village under surveillance."

"Couldn't you have simply arrested them . . . the students and Gamble at least?"

"How could we? We'd not found any ammunition at that point. We had a suspicion . . . but no proof . . . of who did the murder. And you do not approach a person of Sir Edmund's stature and accuse him of incipient revolution on the basis of what some nineteen-year-old student has babbled to you."

"I suppose not."

"Gamble sent some of the students to frighten you out of the cottage, but the papers they brought back were useless to him. He removed the telephone tap before we arrived, but wired the telephone alcove . . . "

"Wired it?"

"Bugged is the usual term. The device enabled Gamble to hear the manor half of all telephone calls. The bug was as small as a shirt button, but picked up the slightest whisper, and everything said in that alcove was recorded efficiently."

"Including my conversation with Beth about Bullock," Michael said.

Whitelaw nodded. "Yes, Mr. Grandville. Bullock was becoming extremely nervous about demonstrations in London scheduled for next week. His previous rallies hadn't been tea parties . . . his own hoodlums used truncheons and bricks. But even Bullock drew the line somewhere. When he realized heavy weapons and grenades would be used . . . then found the London demonstrations would be duplicated in other major cities . . . he became terribly frightened and rushed down here. Bullock's reputation is by now so unsavory that Gamble knew that if you told me of his visit there'd be endless police prying and questions. It was the worst time for that sort of thing, so he altered your car . . . with disastrous results."

"Poor Lily. What a rotten end."

"No more rotten than what Gamble did to her while she was living. We have Benson's word on that."

"Benson too?"

"Certainly."

Michael shifted his weight on the bed and took my hand in his. "How did you *get* all this information from Gamble and Benson, Superintendent?"

"Rather easily, as a matter of fact. They had not considered the possibility of failure, so they were unprepared for it. A common cleft in the criminal mind.

"At any rate, Gamble was merciless with Lily. I gathered she'd encouraged him when he first arrived, then discarded him for Jock Magee. He never got over that. He killed Jock after convincing Sir Edmund that Magee had corrupted Lily. Day and night, here and in London, Gamble kept feeding Lily hints about her father's activities . . . telling her about her accession as a New Age princess.

"Gamble wanted both power and Lily, and he worked to keep her unstable. She'd been giddy . . . spoiled and irresponsible . . . but not a hysteric until Gamble got a hold of her. He goaded her sadistically, told her the uprising was imminent. He had the New Age insignia affixed to a family ring and presented it to Lily as an engagement bond. I understand she threw it at him. The ring ended up in the pocket of a cloak Gamble wore when he darted around the grounds at night . . . "

"And I found it and showed it to Marsden," I said.

"Precisely . . . and Tom Marsden would have done anything to keep Gamble from seeing that ring in the palm of your hand. No explanation would have satisfied Gamble. He'd believe you were in league with the opposition . . . an enemy of the New Age."

"Even so, Superintendent, Marsden certainly had an agitated reaction."

Whitelaw smiled rather inscrutably. "Take my word for it, his motives were pure. When Professor Trehane was killed," he continued, "Lily's worst fears were confirmed. Gamble told her that her father had arranged the murder of his oldest friend. It was the ultimate horror. Lily felt her father was mad . . . that she was going mad herself."

I said, "I think Lily's death was the final blow."

"It was. Sir Edmund couldn't escape the fact that . . . in one way or another . . . he had caused his own daughter's death."

Lily danced through our minds . . . capricious, ethereal.

Whitelaw coughed. "You would both have been next, of course. When people disappear, it's not always obvious right away. It might be late in the week before your colleagues knew you were missing. Then they'd be told you left for London tonight. David Cheney could confirm that you'd talked of the pressures to edit your film, and a sudden departure wouldn't be unreasonable. There'd be a search, but the trail would be cold."

Michael gripped my hand tightly and a question occurred to me. "Michael, speaking of trails, how did you find me?"

"I came back from the accident to find you were missing. I'd just gone out to search when the Superintendent arrived."

"I was in London, mapping strategy," Whitelaw interjected, "when I heard a report of the accident. I flew down right away. Sir Edmund was missing too. My men looked around with no luck, and then we asked Benson. He was uncooperative. Furtive. But Sally came forward and said she had seen Sir Edmund going up the staircase which led to the gallery. That puzzled her, since she knew it was empty and always kept locked. She thought he might want to mourn alone."

"We were just climbing those stairs," Michael said, "when we heard you scream. We shot out the lock." He moved closer to hold me again, and the Superintendent sat unblinkingly through our embrace. When we parted he continued—firmly enough—but his face was bleak and I could see he was desperately tired.

"I told you that Sir Edmund had . . . months ago . . . made a certain decision. It sprung from a probably accurate evaluation that the New Age would get just one chance to succeed. All the ingredients of the overthrow had to be timed to achieve a peak of terror in a particular period.

"The campaign, in fact, had already begun. It began with the death of our Secretary of Defense, Quentin Cooper. Other cabinet ministers and members of Parliament would have followed on a precise schedule. The object was to strip us of leaders, induce hysteria in the people, and bring the government to its knees. While the assassinations were taking place, riots were to be staged in major cities, and bombs exploded on critical roads, bridges, and railway points.

"When the people and government were reeling in turmoil and the moment was right, Littell was prepared to launch another assault. A deadly one. He'd planted fifty cylinders of nerve gas in five British cities."

I caught my breath. "Nerve gas?"

"VX . . . probably the most deadly chemical substance known, and lethal either when inhaled or deposited on the skin. It kills in minutes and contaminates the surrounding area for weeks. Normally VX would be dispersed by plane or rocket, but the New Age group had built fifty bombs . . . ten for each city . . . which would explode the gas cylinders. It wouldn't be as effective as spraying, but that's a subjective, military judgment. Thousands of people would die all the same."

"My God!" Michael said. "We know he was crazy, but this is beyond belief."

"Apparently it was Sir Edmund's plan that only one city be involved at first, and the other bombs held in abeyance as blackmail. Ten students trained for the job and equipped with gas masks and protective suits were stationed in each of the cities. They had an exact scheme for detonating the bombs at various high sites. In *one* of those cities, we're not sure which, the cylinders would actually have been exploded. After a brief wait to let the horror sink in, Littell would have made his proposal for a new government. Made it directly to the people. He'd paint the New Age in glowing terms, of course."

"While threatening the population with nerve gas?"

"The other bombs would be described as a deterrent to the present establishment, not to the man in the street. Sir Edmund would demand the surrender of police and military forces and the resignation of government. If they didn't consent, the other bombs would be exploded, city by city. You can imagine the panic."

"And he thought the people would accept this proposal ... the plan of a monster?"

Whitelaw sighed. "*We* see the fallacy in that lunatic assumption, Mr. Grandville, but Sir Edmund had convinced himself that the people were just waiting to be saved by him ... that they would embrace his new Britain."

"Geoffrey said something like that ...," I murmured.

"Said what, Miss Kendall?"

"That in difficult times people looked for saviors. That people felt helpless to change their own lives and looked for an omnipotent power to do that."

"Basically a sound observation ... but not when the power reigns by terror and anarchy."

"Superintendent, what were his chances?" Michael asked. "*Could* he have pulled it off?"

Whitelaw paused to consider, then answered, "I personally believe that Englishmen everywhere would have risen up and crushed him and his men. With their bare hands if necessary. But along with the deaths from the gas, there would have been terrible bloodshed.

"Benson appears to be having a nervous breakdown. Luckily for us, he's talking steadily as he disintegrates. He gave us Sir Edmund's papers and a list of the bomb sites. That's out of my hands now ... the army is moving on all the locations. By morning the cylinders and the students should be in custody. Must be in custody."

He seemed riddled with anguish. "If we hadn't that list, however, didn't know the locations, what could we have done? Both the gas cylinders and the bomb components could have been carried in an ordinary suitcase. The students could have been anywhere. No, he wouldn't have won in the end . . . but with the gas as a factor, there's no telling what slaughter would have resulted."

The fire snapped as we sat there, dealing with holocaust. Michael broke the spell. "What puzzles me, Superintendent, is the gas itself. Where was it made? Isn't the technology complicated?"

"An hour ago," Whitelaw answered, "I spoke to an army chemist who told me it costs about three pounds or six American dollars to manufacture a quart of VX. A quart contains several million lethal doses.

"Both the English and the U.S. declassified the VX formula in 1971, and after that the British Patent Office actually published two patents on how to make the gas. They were later withdrawn, but by then copies had been distributed to patent libraries throughout the world.

"The Americans have been equally suicidal, placing side-by-side ads in a government journal for manufacturers who could make each of the two VX chemicals. A third ad solicited companies who could fill projectiles with a propellent. It didn't take genius to envision the final binary weapon. The Americans termed the advertisements "unfortunate" and withdrew them, but not before the journal had wide circulation to arms specialists.

"Sir Edmund's gas was made in Marchant's chemical plants in Third World countries. The VX was manufactured behind a screen of some legitimate effort, and in these countries . . . all desperate for capital investment . . . there were no plant inspections. The cylinders were hidden on company planes and brought here by Gamble . . . on what were said to be business flights.

"That's all we know," he stood up, "to this point. I'm sure I don't have to tell you not to speak of this. Not to anyone. The gas should be secured by tomorrow, but it may take weeks to clear all those arms depots, to round up the students . . . and we can't afford leaks. There's no way to hide troop movements and searches, of course, but we'll find some excuse for them.

"Please don't misunderstand me. I'm a believer in the open approach, but this is one exercise where the people *are* better off in the dark." He passed his hand wearily over his eyes. "If we had to deal with mass hysteria in addition to everything else . . . "

Then he picked up his overcoat. "You should be getting some rest now, Miss Kendall. We could all do with some rest."

"Before you leave, Superintendent, I have one final question."

"Yes?"

"You didn't know most of this a few hours ago, when Sir Edmund jumped out that window. If you had known of the gas . . . of his crimes . . . would you have stopped him?"

"To exact retribution, you mean? What would that gain? Who would it help? No, I wouldn't have stopped him. For that crazed and tormented man, it was much the best way."

34

Three days later, Michael and I were leaving Superintendent Whitelaw's rather sterile, square office at Scotland Yard, when Tom Marsden came up. He was huffing and puffing.

"Heard you were here and ran over."

We chitchatted a bit. I was surprised at how ruddily handsome he looked, and how much his forthright smile transformed him.

"Doing the paper work?" he asked. "Signing your statements?"

"Yes," Michael said, "and glad to get it all done. All the unfinished business . . . "

Marsden snapped up a cue. "Speaking of unfinished business, Miss Kendall . . . "

"Yes?"

"May I have my book?"

"Book?"

"*Homage to John Dryden* by T. S. Eliot, published by the Hogarth Press in 1924."

"*Your* book!"

"I'm a clandestine scholar. Yes, my book . . . and now my humblest apologies."

"Then you wrote the note."

"I did."

"But why?"

"I didn't see it myself at first, until the Superintendent . . . ." He fished in his pocket, drew out his wallet, and opened it. "You've not met my wife, Miss Kendall. I'd like you to see a picture of her."

I stared, while Michael threw his head back and laughed. The girl smiling up at me was my twin. Her hair was darker than mine, but her mouth, her nose, her chin . . . all were identical.

"Peas in a pod," Marsden said. "Do you not have any family in Alnick, Miss Kendall?"

I shook my head.

"Or in Elsdon or Alwinton?"

"Not that I know of."

"Back on your family tree, there must be a Northumberland branch. Cousins you've never met."

"Nothing would surprise me at this point. Did you get into trouble for this?"

He made a face. "I was about to. I'd left the note and the book in that cubby the day before Dr. Trehane was killed. I know his murder must have made the note sound really ominous. I'm sorry . . . I didn't mean to frighten you so. I just hoped you'd leave, for your own sake. I had to confess the note to the Superintendent and I thought he was preparing to shoot me. But then he had to rush over to get you out of the cottage, and then the case quickened again . . . and so I got off.

"The Superintendent understood . . . better than I did . . . ," his voice dropped, "why I didn't want you to be hurt. You're so like my Jean, it's uncanny . . . even the way you walk. We've only been married a year, Miss Kendall. Jean means everything to me. I couldn't stand the thought of anything happening to *her*, so I transferred that anxiety to you, and . . . "

I grasped his hand. "Tom, I'm most grateful to you. Really, I . . . " He looked deeply embarrassed. "Thank you, Tom."

"Goodbye, Miss Kendall," his tone was formal again. "Goodbye, Mr. Grandville."

Downstairs, I stood in the London sunshine, enchanted with the burrowing throngs. Michael hailed a cab.

"Where to, sir?"

"The Royal Court."

David Cheney stood on the stage and looked out, shielding his eyes from the glare of the lights. There was an old table at center stage and the actors sat around it, riffling their scripts. David waved, climbed down, and walked up the aisle to us.

"Elizabeth, Michael. How are you?"

"How are you?" Michael asked.

"Keeping busy. Work is the perfect anesthetic, you know."

"Oh David," I said. "I wish . . . "

"Don't wish, Elizabeth," he said stonily. "Wishing is passive. I spent all those months wishing Lily would change, wishing she'd love me . . . I should have picked her up and taken her out of there, taken her away, cherished her just for herself . . . but I wished, instead."

He crossed his arms on the seat in front of him, and put his head down.

Michael let him sit for a moment, then he touched his shoulder. "David, don't torture yourself."

The head was raised. "I try not to. The trouble is . . . it's too soon. I can't shake it yet."

"Can we do anything?"

"Do anything? Yes. Be happy together. Be happy so that something good comes out of this mess."

* * *

In Marylebone, Michael and I spurned the coffeehouse for a bench in Manchester Square. A few blocks away traffic thundered, but the park was hushed in the violet dusk. As we idly watched, people came and went, doors opened and closed, lamps cast their vitelline glow on the walks. I felt all my tension draining away—I was savoring London's great gift of peace.

We'd come from the bookstore, where Michael had led me past shelves and bins to an elderly man who'd produced Lewis Carroll's *A Tangled Tale.*

"To replace Marsden's book," Michael said. "A memento."

In the square I looked down at Frost's pensive dragon, etched in gold on the faded red boards.

"It *has* been just that, hasn't it, Michael?"

"A tangled tale?"

"Yes. A story that began years ago when Sir Edmund was just a child . . . a story which really has no ending."

"Beth . . . "

"With the cross gone, there can't be an ending. I'm sure Philip Atherton has it."

"Maybe not."

"It's just the kind of thing he would do . . . take the cross. He's a fanatic, Michael."

"He'll be caught."

"Perhaps. But perhaps he'll hide the cross first, or pass it along. The cycle will start all over again."

"Not so much gloom, Beth. We have your photograph . . . "

"Blurred."

"I know, I know, but it's *something.* The cross may be found . . . but if it isn't, perhaps we can prove it exists. When this episode can be discussed, the cross will be talked about too."

"Don't you see . . . talk won't help. With the actual cross, the burials could have been dated, Arthur's life proven real. He would have been not just legend, but flesh and bone . . . the man who'd saved England, whose spirit could save it again."

"Perhaps his spirit just did."

I felt my eyes misting. "Oh Michael . . . "

"Beth, it was Geoffrey who found the cross first. Geoffrey who called you. Geoffrey who worked to decipher the legends, to protect our links to those ancient times. Don't you think Arthur's spirit might have been guiding him?"

I had no answer, but I sat there, holding his hand.

In a while he got up. "Come on, love. Let's walk a bit."

We turned right on George Street, then crossed the High Street again, and walked into Marylebone Lane.

"There's just one further development, Beth," Michael said. "I'm scrapping the Thorn Hill sequence."

"Why?"

"Word from on high. They want the whole story squashed until they're sure all the New Age groups have been rounded up. At the inquest this week Sir Edmund's death will be described as an accident."

"When will the truth be told?"

"Not soon. Just now the truth is too dangerous."

We walked further.

"Will you give up the film," I finally asked, "after all your work?"

"Not exactly." I saw he was smiling. "They've found me another subject . . . an Earl this time. He's a genial and uncomplicated fellow, I'm told, with estates in Scotland. It seems I've been endorsed by the government. The British have asked the network, as a kind of diplomatic favor, to give me extra time and increase the budget accordingly."

"And the network's agreed?"

"They're reacting as if I'd been knighted."

We'd reached the cookware store again. The window brimmed with steamers and spoons and the crepe pans gleamed on their racks. The piping tubes and julienne disks stared at me, prim and reproachful. Across the city the Hotel Douglass stood, with my books—and alternatives—stored on its premises. Across the ocean, the Langley School waited.

Michael came close and put up his hand, smoothing my hair. "That's better. I can't bring a tatty bride to Scotland."

"Michael!"

He kissed me. "Right, love. We leave in the morning."